"Don't."
The soft command
lacked authority.

"Don't what, Kate?"

"Don't touch me. Don't make me laugh. Don't make it any harder than it already is for me to fight you."

"Do you have to fight me?" Matt's voice was soft now, too.

She nodded solemnly. "Yes."

"It's a losing battle, you know."

Her eyelids fluttered shut. She knew. She also knew she couldn't afford to lose.

He tilted his head to the side and studied her for a long moment. Then he hugged her close, his husky laugh flowing over her like liquid silk. "Oh, but Kate, just think of all the fun we're going to have when you finally surrender."

Dear Reader:

Summer is here! And we've got six new SECOND CHANCE AT LOVE romances to add to your pleasure in the new season. So sit back, put your feet up, and enjoy . . .

You've also got a lot to look forward to in the months ahead—delightful romances from exciting new writers, as well as fabulous stories from your tried-and-true favorites. You know you can rely on SECOND CHANCE AT LOVE to provide the kind of satisfying romantic entertainment you expect.

We continue to receive and enjoy your letters—so please keep them coming! Remember: Your thoughts and feelings about SECOND CHANCE AT LOVE books are what enable us to publish the kind of romances you not only enjoy reading once, but also keep in a special place and read again and again.

Warm wishes for a beautiful summer,

Ellen Edwards

Ellen Edwards
SECOND CHANCE AT LOVE
The Berkley Publishing Group
200 Madison Avenue
New York, N.Y. 10016

Second Chance at Love®

TOO CLOSE FOR COMFORT

LIZ GRADY

A
SECOND CHANCE AT LOVE
BOOK

To the men in my life:
Bill, Billy, and Ryan

1

IN SPITE OF the two heavy suitcases she was lugging, Kate Lonergan smiled as she crossed the sprawling lawn of what was once the South East lighthouse. As always, the beauty of her family's unusual home, perched high on a cliff overlooking the Atlantic Ocean, enchanted her.

She paused before climbing the porch steps to peer up at the large windows encircling the observation room at the top of the tower. They were black and empty, and Kate tried to shake off the eerie feeling of being watched. Returning to an empty house always made her feel uncomfortable, although in this case she preferred the solitude to its alternative.

It would be much easier to get settled in while her parents were still away on vacation, and with any luck, the quilt shop she planned to open in Block Island's busy Old Harbor district would be alive and kicking by the time they returned from Europe.

The heavy oak door closed behind her with a resounding thud, echoed by two small thumps as she eagerly relinquished the suitcases. Dispensing with her white kid sandals next, Kate wiggled her toes, relishing the feel of the foyer's cool flagstone beneath her feet. Six hours on a jet from the

West Coast and a hot, windy ferry ride over from the port of Narragansett, Rhode Island, had left her feeling an uncomfortable mixture of rumpled, grimy, and exhausted.

Not sure what she wanted most—a cold drink, a chance to wash up, or simply to close her eyes—Kate collapsed on the stairs that wound gracefully to the second floor, content for now to postpone the inevitable moment when she'd have to drag her suitcases up to her room.

She hadn't noticed the steady hum of running water until it stopped suddenly, filling the house with an unnatural silence. Instantly she bolted upright on her perch, listening for a sound, any sound, to break the spell that held her rooted to the step.

"You're imagining it," she said aloud after a few endless moments. She stood, stretching her long legs and hoping that the sound of her own voice would dispel the strange silence. "What you need is a nice long bath, and then bed," she advised herself.

"Sounds inviting."

Kate whirled as the deep voice rumbled from the staircase behind her.

"But I thought Goldilocks wanted supper and a soft bed," the owner of the honey-and-hickory baritone continued. "I don't recall any mention of a long bath in the original version."

His eyes, the deepest blue Kate had ever seen, were full of unbridled amusement. They strayed now, roaming quickly over all five feet six inches of her very tense body, before he spoke again. "But I must admit, I find your addition to the story most intriguing."

Eyes and mouth forming a trio of perfect *O*'s, Kate stared at the impressive male specimen poised above her. He was naked except for a burgundy towel wrapped carelessly around his hips, but for all the self-consciousness he displayed he might as well have been wearing a three-piece suit.

The face surrounding the mesmerizing blue eyes was rugged and weathered in an appealing way. A strong jaw, dark brown mustache sloping slightly to frame full lips, and tiny crinkle lines that appeared at the corners of his eyes when he smiled—as he was now—all contributed to the hard, powerful image he projected. Only those eyes, gleaming like dark sapphires, and his hair, wet and tousled from the shower but still shot through with shafts of amber and gold, softened the impact.

As to a magnet, Kate's gaze was drawn lower, to a well-muscled chest matted with damply curling bronze hairs that narrowed to a silky line over his flat belly before disappearing entirely beneath the towel.

"Pass inspection?" he drawled, obviously enjoying her prolonged scrutiny.

Kate reddened, mortified that he had caught her staring so blatantly. She was also belatedly cognizant of the potential threat the man might pose. As quickly as the hysterical thoughts occurred to her, she rejected them. Common sense told her that murderers, rapists, and even petty thieves, for that matter, seldom paused to grab a shower. More likely he was the boarder her parents were always talking about taking in to keep an eye on the place during their summer jaunts. He looked the strong, capable type who could make their hearts rest easy, but his presence certainly threw a monkey wrench into her plans.

"Who are you?" she demanded, striving to sound calm and in control but managing only a shaky curtness.

"Matt Kincade. Who are you?" He smiled with warm spontaneity, as if he were chatting at a cocktail party. This apparent ease elicited a reflex smile from Kate.

"I'm Kate Lonergan."

He nodded with what seemed to be rather amused recognition. "The rebellious daughter who abandoned her island heritage to get married and traipse off to L.A."

Kate winced. "That colorful rendition of my past could only have come from dear old Mom. I wonder what other tidbits of family history she treated you to over tea and cookies."

His smile was dazzling. "I know you won the state spelling bee three years running, and you were the first one ever to wear a strapless gown to the Block Island senior prom."

"Lucky you." Kate rolled her eyes and heaved a sigh of wry amusement. "Well, as long as you're privy to all the titillating details of my life, perhaps you won't mind answering a few questions for me. For instance, what are you doing here?"

"That one's easy enough: I live here. At least I'll be living here until the end of June, when your folks get back. Next question?"

His friendly smile spread upward to sparkle in the deep blue of his eyes, making it difficult for Kate to concentrate on anything as mundane as an inquisition. Whatever her next question had been, it evaporated under the intense, almost ravishing way he was holding her with his gaze.

Ravishing? What was she thinking? Worse, what was *he* thinking as he stood there smiling serenely, observing her observing him? With great effort, Kate gathered her wandering wits and forced her concentration back to the matter at hand.

"I take it you're renting the lighthouse from my parents until they get back?"

He nodded, and her hopes plummeted. "That's right. Maybe even longer if we keep running into problems out at the site."

"The site?" Kate's eyes narrowed quizzically.

"My construction company is developing a time-sharing resort on the island's north shore," he explained.

A flicker of surprise swept through Kate. She was more out of touch with island news than she'd realized. Most native Block Islanders, herself included, opposed commercial development typified by the sort of resort Matt Kincade was building. But something told Kate this was not the time to alienate him by saying so.

"You're frowning," he observed. "Does that mean you disapprove?"

"I really don't know enough about your project to approve or disapprove," she replied, neatly sidestepping the issue. "At the moment I'm more concerned with the problem facing us here."

"I wasn't aware we had a problem." His blasé expression and nonchalant tone warned Kate she was in for an uphill battle.

"Then you're not very observant, Mr. Kincade." She nodded at the suitcases on the floor beside her. "Have you ever heard of the law of matter that states two objects cannot occupy the same place at the same time?"

His eyes twinkled as he chewed his bottom lip thoughtfully. "It does sound vaguely familiar, and I'd love to stand here and let you quiz me on my college physics, but in view of my...ah...appearance, maybe you'd like to put the rest of your questions on hold for a bit."

His self-assured grin presented Kate with an irresistible challenge. "Why?" she queried with poker-faced innocence. "Is there something unusual about your appearance? I really hadn't noticed." That should dispel any notions he might have that she was standing here drooling over his body.

"Touché." He acknowledged her triumph with a bow of his head, then snatched the victory right out from under her. "Except that charming pink tinge in your cheeks tells me you're very much aware of my appearance."

To her amazement, Kate felt a smile tugging at her lips; her resistance was melting under his gentle teasing.

"But as long as you have no objection to the way I look," he continued, "let's continue playing twenty questions. Only now it's my turn."

He started toward her, moving slowly, almost casually, but there was nothing casual about being approached by a virile stranger wearing only a towel. Kate felt as threatened as if he'd charged down the stairs.

He reached the bottom and stopped, facing her—far too close for Kate's comfort. He seemed broader and taller all of a sudden—at least six feet one or two, Kate estimated as the soft curls on his chest neared her eyes. She would see as much, probably more, if she'd met him on the beach, but under the circumstances, she found the intimate sight very disconcerting.

Tipping her head back, she met his eyes, surprised to find that up close they were more violet than blue and were fringed with thick, dark lashes.

"First question," he said quietly. "What are you doing here unannounced?" As Kate watched, fascinated, his strong, tapered fingers briefly lifted a curl of tawny gold from her shoulder. "Besides playing Goldilocks, that is."

"Easy: I live here." Somehow she managed to glibly toss his own reply back at him despite the fluttery numbness that pervaded every cell of her body at his light touch.

Smiling skeptically, he traced the lines of her body with his gaze. It was a painstakingly unhurried perusal, lingering on each swell and hollow in turn, and Kate swore she could feel the heat of it right through the fabric of her sundress. That he was vividly imagining what lay beneath the soft blue cotton was obvious from the enjoyment he made no effort to conceal.

"Impossible," he announced finally, dragging his attention back to her flushed face. "You can't live here. I'm sure I'd remember if I'd ever bumped into you in the shower."

His steamy glances and slightly suggestive remarks were as out of line as the sensations they sent sizzling through her, but he managed to deliver it all with such a light, good-natured touch that Kate found herself laughing along.

"That's probably because I always use the shower on the deck out back," she retorted, matching his bantering tone.

"I see." A look of mock ferociousness settled on his face, his eyes narrowing accusingly. "Are you the one who's been swiping all the peanut butter?"

"Never touch the stuff," she answered, shaking her head for emphasis.

"In that case, you can stay."

Again they laughed, and Kate was caught up in the rough, inordinately pleasing sound of his laugh and the disarming grin he flashed her. Then the full implication of his pronouncement hit her.

"I plan on staying," she informed him, searching for a tactful way to broach the rest of the problem and failing. "You're the one who'll be leaving."

"Now why would I want to do that?" He sounded neither surprised nor angry, simply interested.

"Because," she explained hurriedly, "this is my home, and I'll be living here this summer. I guess I should have called my folks and told them about my plans, but I was afraid if I did they'd cancel their trip. I had no idea they'd actually found someone to rent the lighthouse."

"I understand," he assured her. "It's no problem."

Kate could feel the tension easing out of her and gratitude taking its place. She hadn't expected him to make it so easy.

"Thank you. I realize my thoughtlessness has inconvenienced you, so please, take a few days to find another place. Luckily the tourist season hasn't started yet. After Memorial Day, rooms on the island will be as scarce as hen's teeth."

He raised his hand with a laugh. "Whoa, slow down. When I said there was no problem, I meant I had no objection to your moving in—even though my agreement with your folks was for me to have the entire lighthouse to myself."

Kate stared at him, hearing but not believing. "Move in? You mean with you? Me and you together?"

He shrugged carelessly, but she could tell by the barely restrained twitching of his mustache that he was suppressing laughter. "Why not? There's plenty of room."

"There are a lot of reasons why not. Number one being that I know nothing about you—except that you have the gall to stand there in a towel and carry on a conversation with a perfect stranger."

He swept a critical—and, Kate, would wager, experienced—eye over the now well-explored terrain of her body, tilting his head in an exaggerated manner of appraisal.

"You're a looker all right, Kate. But perfect?" His tenuous control over the laughter slipped, permitting a chuckle to escape. "I don't think even I'd go that far."

Kate glared at him. "If that's an example of your manners—or should I say your complete lack of them?—I wouldn't share a taxi with you, much less my home."

To Kate's surprise, he had the good grace to look sheepish. "You're right. I apologize for my rudeness, and I promise it won't happen again."

She managed to maintain a disdainful expression, but his seemingly heartfelt remorse took most of the angry wind out of her sails. While she was still trying to figure out what tack to take next, he continued.

"There are some other things we should get settled if we're going to be roommates, but as you just pointed out, I'm not dressed properly for a discussion with a stranger." He hooked one sunbrowned finger under her chin. "Perfect or otherwise. So, while I slip into something that will make you more comfortable, why don't you start dinner? I lit the grill before showering, so the coals should be just about right by now. The steaks are in the refrigerator."

Kate met his eyes with an air of determination, ignoring the backhanded dinner invitation. "I'm not going to be your roommate."

"We'll talk about it over dinner," he countered, telling

her with his eyes that, at the moment, that was as far as he was willing to compromise. "Otherwise I won't even be able to hear you with my stomach growling. Didn't you ever hear that the way to get rid of a man is through his stomach?"

Laughing in spite of herself, Kate decided to play along—temporarily. "I think you've got that twisted, but at this point I'm willing to try anything."

"Anything?" he echoed provocatively. Fortunately, he had the wisdom not to elaborate. Bolting up the stairs two at a time, he tossed back over his shoulder, "I like mine rare."

"Figures," Kate muttered under her breath.

She sensed that lurking beneath Matt Kincade's easygoing demeanor were the instincts of a born predator. It was a quality she was familiar with; she'd seen enough of it during her marriage to Jeff to last her two lifetimes.

Fortunately, she wasn't without a certain amount of cunning herself. Making a short detour to the pantry, she selected a bottle of rosé from her father's well-stocked wine rack. A smile of satisfaction curved her lips as she noted the vintage, and when she headed for the kitchen she was humming with cheerful self-confidence. If music had powers to soothe the savage breast, there was no telling what miracles dinner and a few glasses of good wine might work.

One way or another, Matt Kincade was about to be persuaded to see things her way.

2

THE COALS WERE white-hot, perfect for the thick steaks Kate selected. Aside from the supply of steak—enough to rebuild a small cow—there was precious little in the refrigerator. Which was probably just as well. The frozen french fries and biscuits she eventually unearthed from the deepest recesses of the freezer were as much of a culinary challenge as she could handle.

She set the table in the sun-room off the kitchen with her mother's earthenware, then slipped into the bathroom to freshen up. She dreaded that first glance in the mirror, fervently hoping she didn't look as wilted as she felt. Miraculously, her hair and dress seemed to have survived the long trip in better shape than her spirits had.

For a moment she considered following Matt's example and changing into something more comfortable, but she decided against it. Her comfort, or discomfort, this evening had nothing whatsoever to do with what she was wearing.

She made it back to the deck just as the steaks were ready for flipping. Unfortunately, by that time the fries and rolls were slightly past their prime. When Matt strolled into the cozy yellow and white kitchen a few minutes later, she was hastily arranging them in napkin-lined baskets, trying to make sure the best ones ended up on top.

Nothing in twenty-seven years of living had prepared Kate for the liquid weakness that invaded her limbs at the mere sight of Matt Kincade in snug, faded jeans and a blue cotton shirt partially, and enticingly, unbuttoned. His bare feet added a touch of intimacy to the scene.

"I put your suitcases in the room at the top of the stairs. Is that okay?" He snatched a fry from the basket and blew on it to cool it off.

"Good guess. That's my old room."

"I could tell."

Kate didn't know which was more tantalizing, the fresh scent of his cologne or the mischievous gleam in his eyes. Before she had a chance to ask just how he could tell, he reached for the steak platter, brushing her fingers in the process and spurring her pulse from a race to a gallop.

"Mmm, this looks delicious." He nodded at the baskets of too-crisp french fries and slightly charred rolls. "Did you make a salad?"

His sincere appreciation of her efforts, coupled with the beguilingly hopeful question, melted Kate's heart.

"With what?" she asked, counting on sarcasm to hide her reluctant attraction to him. "The soggy tomato and slimy lettuce I found in the vegetable bin?"

He shrugged, undaunted by her implied criticism of his housekeeping. "I figured maybe you'd come up with something."

"Why? Because I happen to be a woman?"

A look scorching enough to rival the coals out back came into his eyes. "Lady, you don't just happen to be a woman. You're one hundred percent woman, and you do a better job of it than anyone I've ever seen."

Again he stole her thunder with a few golden words and the mystical power of his eyes.

"Well, anyway," Kate returned a little anticlimactically and so quickly she sounded almost breathless, "cooking is not a sex-linked characteristic."

Matt's eyes glittered devilishly. "I suppose not. But who would have thought I could draw you into a discussion of sex this early in the evening? Things look promising."

"Just eat," she ordered.

He obeyed—with gusto—polishing off his steak and helping himself to seconds of the fries. At the same time he neatly evaded her increasingly less subtle attempts to persuade him to find accommodations elsewhere.

When the last bit of roll had disappeared into his mouth, he reclined in the fan-back wicker chair with an expectant smile.

"Don't tell me." Kate shook her head in disbelief. "You want to know what's for dessert."

His bright gaze held hers, never wavering, an X-rated smile on his lips. "I already know what I want for dessert. But first let's settle this other little problem you say we have. I'll tell you what I've decided to do as soon as we get these dishes done. Do you want to wash or dry?"

He was already on his feet, collecting silverware and haphazardly stacking dishes.

"Neither," Kate replied. "I cooked, remember?"

"Suit yourself. It'll just be that much longer until you hear my decision."

She sighed resignedly. "I'll dry."

Matt proved to be an exuberant dishwasher, getting as much soapy water on them as on the dishes. Humming tunelessly, he rinsed each dish with meticulous care, oblivious to the impatient tapping of Kate's foot.

"I think I'll finish my wine out on the deck," he announced when the last dish had been put away, leaving Kate no choice but to follow him.

They sat on the steps, Matt leaning back to rest his elbows on the step behind them and stretching his long legs out in front. The movement pressed his muscular thigh against Kate's, instantly sabotaging her plan to remain stone sober and in control of the situation. She felt as light-headed and dizzy as if she'd polished off the wine all by herself.

From their vantage point at the tip of the island, the evening sky was a panoramic expanse of black velvet, broken only by a silver sprinkling of stars.

For a long time the only sound was the muffled roar of the surf rushing onto the secluded beach below. The rhythmic pounding underscored the intimacy of the setting.

"So when are you leaving?" Kate prodded when it became apparent Matt was not going to take the initiative.

He turned his head to meet her eyes steadily, his mustache lifting above a smug grin. "I'm not. Not tonight or in a few days or even in a couple of weeks. Not, as I told you earlier, until my work on the island is completed."

The spirit of playfulness she'd already come to expect from him was nowhere in sight now. His eyes were still friendly, but Kate could detect girders of steel determination beneath their dark blue lights. She could almost hear all her well-planned arguments fizzling, burned out by the sheer intensity of the man sitting next to her.

"You have to go!" she burst out in frustration.

"Of course I don't. I have a lease on this place, which is more than you can say."

Kate's chin came up. "I don't need a lease. This is my parents' home. And they never would have signed your foolish lease if they'd known I was coming home."

"Then why didn't you tell them?"

His deep, cool drawl only fueled her anger. "I already told you: I didn't want to spoil their vacation and—oh, why am I even bothering to explain anything to you? You really intend to stay here even though you're not wanted, don't you? Nothing I say or do is going to change your mind."

He shook his head slowly, resolutely. If he smiled, she'd clobber him.

"Nothing. Not the wine you so obligingly keep pouring nor your earnest attempts to convince me I'd be happier elsewhere—not even those big green eyes that threaten to drown me if I stare into them for too long."

"Why?"

His gaze shifted back to the night-darkened ocean. "Because I like it here. It's quiet, private, and a heck of a lot better than living in a trailer out at the site. But even if the lighthouse were as uncomfortable as one of those trailers, I'd still stay, as long as I could share it with you."

"That's really what this is all about, isn't it!" Kate exploded. "You've got some adolescent fantasy about living here with me because I'm a woman."

He smiled, a devastating smile that curled the dark mustache and crinkled the lines at the corners of his eyes. "I haven't really had time to fully develop my fantasies about you yet, but I can assure you they'll be anything but adolescent."

Kate felt the fire creep up her neck to her cheeks, and she knew the heat wasn't generated by embarrassment alone.

"You had that one coming," Matt hastened to point out before she recovered enough to vent the fury that had started bubbling inside. "And you can stop looking so aghast. Despite my admittedly lascivious fantasies, brute force has never been my way with women." He stroked his chin thoughtfully. "I wonder about you, though. Did the sight of my near nakedness get you so hot and bothered that you're afraid you won't be able to control yourself if we live here together?"

"My self-control is the least of my worries, Mr. Kincade." Frost formed on the reply as it left her mouth.

"Good." He heaved an exaggerated sigh of relief. "It's reassuring to know I'm not in danger of being compromised."

"The only thing you're in danger of is being arrested for trespassing when I call the police and explain the situation."

It was a childish threat; still, Kate's palm itched to remove the tauntingly smug grin from his face.

"Let me spare you the embarrassment. Before I turned one shovelful of soil for the resort I'm building here, I made it a point to learn everything there is to know about leases and rental agreements. The one your folks and I signed is ironclad."

Kate's shoulders slumped. There was no doubt in her mind that he was telling the truth about his right to stay. That meant her situation had just slipped from troublesome to desperate. He wouldn't leave, and she couldn't. All the cash she could lay her hands on was tied up in stock for the new shop, and her only relatives on the island, her sister and brother-in-law, lived in a small cottage already overflowing with kids and pets.

"C'mon, Kate." The deep voice had taken on a husky, cajoling quality. "There's plenty of room here for the two of us, and if you're honest you'll admit you'd be a whole lot safer with me to protect you than you would be living way out here alone."

"Assuming I need protecting, why should I trust you to do it? I don't even know you."

"But you know your parents, and they trusted me enough to allow me into their home. That has to count for something."

Recalling her folks' almost fanatical concern for their lighthouse, Kate silently agreed that it did indeed count for something.

Clearly interpreting her silence as a sign she was weakening, Matt accelerated his efforts to convince her. "Besides, it'll only be for a few weeks."

"Six weeks," interjected Kate.

He shrugged. "So it's a few more than a few. I'm out at the site all day and sometimes most of the night. And from what you told me over dinner about the work involved in opening a quilt shop, you'll be pretty busy yourself." He flashed a beguiling smile. "Maybe you'll get lucky and our paths will never cross."

Kate regarded him witheringly. "Somehow I can't imagine you'd let me get that lucky."

He chuckled. "You're right. I wouldn't. I fully intend to pursue you, Kate. I decided that the instant I saw you sprawled so charmingly on those stairs."

"Couldn't you just pursue me from afar?" she asked wistfully.

"Nope. Your being under the same roof will make the chase that much easier, but I will promise to respect your privacy. Contrary to what this first impression has probably led you to believe, I'm not generally an obnoxious person— just a fairly desperate one at the moment."

"That's funny," she said darkly, "I'm feeling a little desperate myself right now."

"You won't be for long. You won't be feeling desperate, or over-stressed or burned-out or any of those other things it's so trendy to feel. I'm going to see to it that you're very happy here, Kate."

"You can make me deliriously happy right now; say you'll leave."

He shook his head and smiled. "That wouldn't make you as happy as my staying is going to make you. Now all I have to do is convince you that you can be happy here . . . with me."

"I plan on being very happy here—without any help from you."

"Are you sure about that? Block Island is a long way from L.A., Kate, and decidedly lacking in the glitter and glamour it looks like you've become accustomed to."

His gaze was faintly critical as it surveyed the sleek lines of her designer sundress. This time Kate suspected he was appraising the price of the garment and not its contents, and she found herself on the defensive.

"I realize that my life here on the island won't be as glamorous or exciting as it was in California," she explained. "But that's exactly why I decided to come home. It took five years of that madness to teach me that I want a simple life, simple things."

"Simple?" The blunt speculation in his voice was echoed by his raised brows. "Like that outfit you're wearing? And the fancy leather luggage I hauled up to your room? I bet you don't own anything that doesn't have a designer label on it."

That stung. Kate straightened with sudden intent fierceness. "What I wear and what I own are none of your business."

"Yet."

"Ever." She heard her voice rising and consciously lowered it an octave. "If I'm so bourgeois and decadent, why are you so hell-bent on living here with me?"

He stared at her, openly bewildered. "Damned if I know. You're cool, polished, very L.A. I look at you and see everything I don't want in a woman. And yet, I want you more than I can ever remember wanting a woman in my life."

Kate's breath caught at the hunger in his soft tone. "You don't even know me."

"I wasn't aware that was a prerequisite. I guess I have unorthodox hormones." His wicked grin held an unnerving masculine promise.

"What you have is a serious personality disorder: You're out of your mind. And I'm too tired to sit here and argue with a crazy man. Good night."

Matt's hand clamped onto her thigh before she could spring to her feet. The touch of his fingers was molten, burning through the fabric of her dress, making her heart race, and setting her senses reeling. It was an alarming reaction, and one totally at odds with the resentment she was feeling.

"Does that mean you're staying here with me?" he asked softly.

"It means I have no choice—for tonight."

"That's progress, anyway."

"Don't look so damned triumphant. There has to be a way to get rid of you, and I fully intend to find it. Enjoy the view . . . while you still can." She pushed his hand off her leg and stood, only to find herself face to face with him, his big body between her and the safe haven of the house.

"Aren't you forgetting something?" He lifted his arms to rest them on her shoulders, lacing his fingers behind her neck and leaning closer.

Kate felt her pulse leap wildly as nervous anticipation swept through her. "What are you doing?" she asked tremulously, watching his mouth lower and knowing perfectly well what he was doing.

"Having my dessert," he breathed just before his lips touched hers.

Kate's first impulse was to resist, but in a fraction of a second the warmth and sweetness of the lips brushing tentatively over hers stole her will to do so. It was immediately obvious that Matt had no intention of rushing the kiss, that he intended to take—and give—full pleasure.

He slid his hands down to stroke her back tenderly while the moist tip of his tongue memorized the shape of her mouth. It flicked gently, excruciatingly, and Kate told herself she would call a halt . . . soon.

Then the kiss deepened, taking on a new dimension as her lips parted to accept a taste of heaven from his. What had started as a whim became compulsion, their bodies instinctively straining against each other. One strong hand moved to the small of her back to urge her impossibly closer. Kate felt the smooth muscles of his shoulders move beneath her fingers, felt the heat and strength of hard thighs pressed against hers.

His mustache brushed softly against her skin as his lips wandered to taste her cheek and the tender skin at the side of her neck, then returned to claim her mouth once more. This time Kate moved her tongue, at first hesitantly, then with a sureness spurred by the responsive groan deep in his throat.

Matt permitted her to search his mouth, to taste the essence of him for long, blissful moments, before he took the initiative once more. His lips were like satin, sliding over hers deftly, languorously, preparing her for the provocative thrust of his tongue. Kate felt his hand burning a path up from her hip until his palm rested lightly over her ribs. His fingers played them gently, stroking, kneading, always gliding higher.

Now it was Kate whose hormones were behaving in an unorthodox fashion, urging him on even though she knew the bold, intimate touch he was building toward would cause her to withdraw. But that awkward moment never materialized. Whether he sensed her slight, instinctive stiffening or was simply a master of seductive timing, his fingers stopped their ascent just below her breast, supporting the small, firm swell but not claiming it.

When they were both breathless, he took his mouth from hers, expelling a long, ragged sigh that told Kate a great deal about the effect the kiss had had on him. Through dazed eyes she watched as he slowly licked his lips, clearly savoring the taste of her that lingered on them.

"Mmm, best dessert I've ever tasted."

To Kate, the soft words were a taunting reminder of their conflict. Humiliated, she realized she had just engaged in love-play with a man who was not only not her lover, but who was actually more enemy than friend.

"Well, savor it," she snarled, jerking away from him, "because I don't plan to be on the menu again."

At some point during the night, long after Matt's footsteps had echoed on the winding stairs to the tower room and before the pink light of dawn filtered through the white ruffled curtains, it had occurred to Kate that the best way to handle this crisis was to share it. Once she'd made up her mind to pool brainpower with her sister, Meg, and brother-in-law, Dave, first thing in the morning, she'd finally been able to relax.

In the hazy moments of near sleep that had followed, her mind had filled with the memory of the kiss she and Matt had shared. It *had* been shared; Kate was too honest not to admit it. Lying there in her dark and silent room, the magical sensations produced by his warm lips and callused fingertips had seemed to surge to life once more, ushering her into a sweet and surprisingly peaceful sleep.

Now she was eager to be on her way. She showered quickly, conquering the immature urge to dump the masculine shaving gear on the bathroom shelf into the wastebasket. Dressed in shorts and a cool top in anticipation of a warm day, she headed downstairs. So far there had been no sight or sound of her unwanted roommate, but the aroma of freshly perked coffee wafting from the kitchen told her he was up and about.

After last night she wouldn't eat so much as a slice of bread belonging to him, but the coffee smelled too tempting to pass up. If he made one snide remark, she'd simply toss a quarter in his face . . . and immensely enjoy doing it.

The kitchen was blessedly empty. She took a mug from the cupboard and started to pour coffee, then froze at the sound of his rough drawl.

"Hello, Goldilocks. You sure look happy this morning." Kate twirled in time to see his gaze move appreciatively over her yellow shorts and white halter top. "Pretty, too."

She hadn't noticed him when she walked in because he was standing in a small alcove off the kitchen that served as a laundry room. He was leaning casually against the wall, clad only in a pair of white briefs that molded and defined what yesterday's towel had left to her imagination.

"How long have you had these exhibitionist tendencies?" she inquired sarcastically, trying to ignore the wide expanse of tanned masculine flesh that was making her blood run thick and hot.

He shrugged with the arrogance Kate was quickly coming to recognize as a major character flaw. "What can I say?

I'm not used to living with a prude."

"A situation that is very easily remedied." She smiled pointedly. "Move out."

"I think I'd rather just put on my pants." He tapped the top of the softly rumbling dryer. "As soon as they're dry."

Kate turned back to her coffee, silently cursing when Matt ambled over to lounge against the counter, close beside her, making it a challenge just to draw a steady breath.

"I can't seem to get the hang of this whole domestic routine," he confided, as if she cared. "If I get the grocery shopping done, I let the laundry slide. And if I manage to get to the wash before I run out of clean everything, I forget something else."

"My heart bleeds for you," she snapped, brushing past him to sit at the kitchen table.

"That's another reason we'll make ideal roommates," he went on, trailing after her. "We could divide up the chores around here. You could handle the cooking and cleaning"— his smile deepened provocatively—"and I could do what I'm good at."

Disbelief mingled with disdain in Kate's brain. "In your dreams."

"I already have, believe me."

She felt herself blushing at the soft proclamation and was furious with herself. Matt sat down across from her, cutting the visual distractions in half; now all she had to ignore was the sight of his broad, tanned chest.

"It's obvious you don't welcome my presence here any more this morning than you did last night," he observed.

"How astute of you to notice."

"I notice everything about you," he declared quietly. "As a matter of fact, I have a proposition for you."

Her gasp was automatic. She slammed her mug onto the table so hard that coffee sloshed over its rim. "I'm not interested in any proposition you might make."

Matt smiled mysteriously. "Even if it means I could be out of here in twenty-four hours?"

"In that case, I'm all ears."

His chuckle had a cynical overtone. "I thought that'd get your attention. The proposition is simple. I can't very well find another place to live on a Sunday, but if you still want me to leave in the morning, I'll go peacefully."

Kate eyed him cautiously. "I don't know what to say."

"Don't say anything yet. I still have twenty-four hours to win a place in your heart."

The cocky self-confidence in his grin told Kate he considered that ample time. So that was his game. Gleefully, she realized she couldn't lose. Once the Lonergan will of iron was invoked, it would take more than twenty-four hours and one overbearing male to break it.

"I can see you accept my terms," he said dryly.

"With pleasure."

He leaned forward. "Good. Now that that's out of the way, what should we do today?"

The nerve of the man! He acted as if their spending the day together was a foregone conclusion. No doubt this was all part of his ploy to win her over. Kate weighed her response carefully, not wanting to shoot him down so abruptly he got angry and withdrew his proposal, and not wanting to spend the day with him either. A small voice inside reminded her that she might be more vulnerable to some types of his persuasion than she wished.

She finally decided that sticking to her original plan was the safest way out. She crossed to the sink and rinsed her mug, then turned to him with a sweet smile.

"Thanks for offering to keep me company, but I plan to visit my sister and her family today. I haven't seen them in almost a year."

To her amazement, Matt nodded enthusiastically. "That's fine with me. I've been so busy I haven't had a chance to stop and see the kids all week."

"The kids?" Kate echoed in confusion.

"Your sister's kids," he explained as if she were a not-so-bright-child. "Danny, Kathleen, and Brian. Remember?" While she was still trying to figure out the significance of his familiarity with her family, Matt extracted a pair of jeans and a red T-shirt from the dryer and proceeded to dress in front of her.

She watched, unwillingly mesmerized as he thrust first one long leg and then the other into the jeans. Her gaze trailed his fingers as he zipped the zipper and snapped the snap. He slipped his feet into a pair of comfortable-looking deck shoes and lifted laughing blue eyes to meet hers.

His expression a blend of amusement and challenge, he announced, "I'm ready whenever you are."

By the time they were bouncing along Mohegan Trail to Meg's house in Matt's old but relatively clean pickup, Kate had convinced herself to look on the bright side and try to enjoy the day.

After all, she had won the war—or was about to. By this time tomorrow she'd have the lighthouse all to herself. And while Kate had no intention of cooperating with Matt's announced plans to pursue her, she couldn't deny that he was an attractive and personable man. At least he was attractive and personable when he wasn't being arrogant and overbearing.

Besides, this afternoon would be spent on her territory, with her family for allies. She'd like to see him try his seduction routine with her two-hundred-pound brother-in-law standing guard and three active kids crawling all over her.

As they turned onto Sandy Lane and the white cottage came into view, Kate became too excited to worry about Matt Kincade's intentions. She was glad she'd kept her homecoming a secret. She couldn't wait to see the expressions on the kids' faces when they learned Aunt Kate would be here for the whole summer—maybe even permanently if the new shop was a financial success.

The truck had barely rolled to a halt when Kate was leaping out. She was halfway up the brick walk, a bag of presents slung over her shoulder like Santa's pack, when the screen door swung open and the baby, twenty-month-old Brian, charged out.

"Brian!" Kate exclaimed, her heart swelling at the smile of sheer adoration that lit his baby face.

She'd expected an enthusiastic greeting from Danny and Kathleen but had feared Brian was too young to remember her from last summer. Crouching down, she spread her arms wide and watched his chubby little legs propel him closer and closer...and straight past her as, with a squeal of delight, her tiny nephew hurled himself into the waiting arms of Matt Kincade.

3

HARD ON BRIAN'S heels came the rest of the O'Hara clan, descending on Kate with all the hoopla she'd anticipated.

Her sister Meg waited on the porch steps, hands firmly planted on slim hips, shaking her short, sandy curls but smiling from ear to ear.

"Kate, you sneak! Why didn't you let us know you were coming home?"

Laughing, Kate skipped up the steps and gave her a quick hug. "Because I wanted to surprise you." Holding the oversized shopping bag aloft, she added, "And speaking of surprises . . ."

Seven-year-old Danny and five-year-old Kathleen squealed with knowing delight.

"What did you bring us this time, Aunt Kate?"

"I want to see, too."

"It's not polite to ask someone—" Meg was lecturing in what Kate's brother-in-law, Dave, referred to as her meanmother voice, when Dave broke in, tugging playfully on Kate's arm.

"Me too, Aunt Kate! What did you bring me?"

Meg raised her hands in exasperation. "I give up. Let's see what's in the goody bag."

A half hour later they were settled around the picnic table out back, surrounded by a sea of crumpled wrapping paper, sipping homemade lemonade. When the last toy and Los Angeles Dodgers T-shirt had been pulled from the bag, Matt turned to Kate with a pout as phony as a three-dollar bill.

"You didn't bring me a present?"

For the sake of the children who obviously thought "Uncle Matt" walked on water, she refrained from telling him what she'd like to give him. "Hardly, when I had no way of knowing you'd even be here."

"Don't worry, I'm sure I'll think of some way for you to make it up to me."

Kate saw Meg and Dave exchange a surprised smile, and she knew what they were thinking: exactly what Matt's smooth tone and twinkling eyes had led them to think. So much for relying on the home-court advantage.

Ignoring his silly, expectant grin, she reached for one of the tiny figures Brian was busy lining up on the table in front of him. He was still nestled in the sanctuary of Matt's lap, his curly-blond head resting against the red T-shirt as he methodically removed and replaced the pilot and passengers from his new toy plane.

"Brian, would you like to come sit with me and I'll tell you all about the real big plane I rode on yesterday?"

"No."

The one word held all the awesome defiance of an almost-two-year-old. Kate bit her lip, knowing it was stupid to feel hurt but feeling it all the same.

"Enjoy it, Kate," advised Meg. "An hour from now he'll have warmed up, and you'll be begging him for a moment's peace."

"I don't know about that, Meg," Matt chimed in. "They say kids and dogs have a sort of sixth sense about people."

Meg whacked playfully at his shoulder. "Oh, honestly, Matt. Quit teasing her."

All heads turned in unison as a slight disagreement between Danny and Kathleen erupted into a full-fledged sibling skirmish, complete with hysterical cries and threats of violence.

"That's my cue," Meg groaned, jumping up and crossing the yard to the battle site. "Okay, you two, cool out, or no TV for a week."

"But, Mom, she . . ."

"He . . ."

With a weary shrug, Dave heaved his husky frame from the chaise longue. "I guess I'd better light the grill. The natives tend to get a little restless around feeding time."

When he'd ambled away, leaving Matt and Kate alone with Brian, Matt turned to her.

"Go ahead, let me have it," he invited.

"I don't know what you're talking about."

"Just say whatever it is that's making steam pour out of your ears. It would be a lot healthier than grinding those pearly whites that probably cost your folks a bundle in orthodontist bills."

"I never went to an orthodontist."

"Ah, you're a natural beauty."

"And you're a natural—"

"Ah ah ah, not in front of the children."

"Ahah, not in fwont of the chilwin," echoed Brian, making her grit her teeth all over again.

"Didn't anyone ever tell you that blood is thicker than water?" she demanded of the baby, who only chortled up at Matt and tugged at his mustache.

As if to further disprove her words, Danny and Kathleen chose that moment to brush past her in a race to reach Matt first.

Danny held up a short length of rope. "You said the next time you came you'd show us the bowline knot. Will you, Matt?"

"Please, Uncle Matt," entreated Kathleen.

"I used to be a Boy Scout," he explained to Kate, a tantalizing innocence in his voice.

She shot him a look that spoke volumes about her opinion of him as loyal, honest, and trustworthy, and said sweetly, "Truth is stranger than fiction."

"C'mon, Matt," prodded Danny, shifting impatiently from one foot to the other.

Swinging Brian easily to the ground, Matt jumped up.

"Okay, troop, for today's lesson, first the bowline, then the half-clove. Now all I need is a victim—I mean, a volunteer—to demonstrate the efficiency of my technique."

His gaze came to rest on Kate, moving down her body as slowly as a caress, and it was a full moment before she realized exactly what he was suggesting.

"Forget it," she snapped. "There's no way I'm going to let you tie me up."

"No?" He met her gaze with a blend of longing and disappointment that was miles over the heads of the children. His tone grew wistful. "Perhaps some other time."

They were off then, scrambling down a gentle slope to the lower part of the yard, where the kids circled around Matt with expressions of rapt attention. Kate watched the scene, puzzled. It took time and patience and something more—genuineness?—to merit that kind of trust from children. In that, at least, she agreed with Matt. Kids often displayed an uncanny ability to weed out the good guys from the bad.

Could that mean she was wrong about Matt? After all, he wasn't exactly a bad guy, just annoyingly persistent, and certainly all wrong for her. She watched as he completed the first knot and held it up to the approving shouts of his audience. He tugged the intricate web of rope tighter, and even from where she sat Kate could see the smooth wave of muscles working in his upper arms. The sight of the red shirt stretched snugly across his chest prompted the memory of how that same chest looked *sans* T-shirt. Lean and hard and brown. She felt a sudden flutter of desire, a sensation so physical it was difficult to ignore.

"He's something, isn't he?" Meg plopped a pan of fresh corn on the picnic table.

"Hmm?" murmured Kate, being purposely obtuse. "Oh, you mean Matt. Well, the kids sure seem to like him."

"Adore him, you mean. And why not? To them he's Luke Skywalker and Superman all rolled into one."

The very last thing Kate wanted was to discuss the glowing attributes of Matt Kincade. She reached for an ear of corn and automatically began peeling off the rough, green outer skin and the moist, silky threads beneath. Its aroma drifted up to her, sweet and fresh, a smell from summers past.

"Have you heard from Mom and Dad?" she asked Meg.

Meg tossed another husked ear into the pan; that made four to Kate's one. "Let's see, I got a letter from them last Monday. They were somewhere on the coast of Wales, and

Mom had just discovered a fountain that's the perfect setting for her big love scene. Has she mentioned to you if this next book is a contemporary or a historical?"

Kate chuckled. "A contemporary, I hope. I don't think people made love in fountains two hundred years ago."

"You mean they do today?"

"You're asking the wrong person." Kate's stiffening was slight, but not so slight a sister who was also a best friend would miss it.

"That hardly sounds like the gay divorcée talking."

"Well, maybe this divorcée isn't so gay." Kate saw the look of concern that formed on Meg's face and smiled reassuringly. "Relax. I'm not as bitter as that may have sounded. I'm not bitter at all, actually, just . . ." She searched for the right adjective and reluctantly settled on "confused."

Confused? Where had that come from? Yesterday she'd boarded a plane the epitome of confidence and determination, totally focused on turning this new shop—and her life—into a dazzling success. So since when had she become confused? The answer was unavoidable. Since Matt.

Matt. Without command or will, her eyes strayed in his direction. He'd stripped off his shirt while she was busy shucking corn, but if its removal made him feel cooler, it had the opposite effect on Kate. Before she could sort out the hows and whys of all the feelings he stirred in her, Meg intruded on her thoughts.

"That's as good a reason to feel confused as I've ever seen."

"Don't be silly. He's not my type."

"That, my dear"—Meg nodded at Matt, now assisting Danny in a cartwheel—"is every woman's type."

"Not mine," Kate reiterated firmly. "He's too much like Jeff."

Meg searched her eyes. For what? Kate wondered. Signs of pain? Regret? She wouldn't find them. The only thing she'd felt when her divorce had become final eight months ago was relieved. And free, and a whole lot wiser than the twenty-three-year-old who'd traipsed so starry-eyed into marriage.

"Jeff?" Meg sounded incredulous. "Matt's not at all like Jeff, Kate."

"Maybe not overtly," Kate acknowledged, "but the potential is there. He may not be as polished as Jeff, or as powerful . . . yet, but he's every bit as ambitious and ruthless. Believe me, marriage to Jeff made me an expert on that type of man."

Meg shook her head and tossed the final ear of corn into the pan. "You're wrong about Matt. Just give him a chance."

"No," Kate replied quickly, too quickly. "I may be wrong about Matt, but I'm not wrong about my feelings. And I'm telling you that blue eyes and lots of well-arranged muscle tissue are not incentive enough to risk getting involved with a man like that again."

Her tone was disdainful, but the eyes that traced Matt's romping movements across the yard were not.

"Yeah?" Meg stood and lifted the pan of corn. "Well, if you want to know what I think, I think you doth protest too much. Talk to me again after you two have lived in the lighthouse for a while together."

"We won't be—"

Before she could finish explaining their strange bargain, Dave shouted, "Let's cut the chatter and get that corn cooking. These coals are ready and waiting."

"Yes, sir," Meg replied, rolling her eyes at Kate. "Want to give me a hand in the kitchen?"

Kate was happy to let the conversation shift from Matt, even if her thoughts wouldn't. They talked about the kids, her plans for the shop, about Dave's first year as principal of the island's small school, and all the while Kate ferried an assortment of picnic paraphernalia out back, on each trip sneaking a look at Matt. It was going to take a lot of concentrated thought to figure out why she was so attracted to a man who was so obviously wrong for her.

All she wanted was a man who was gentle and loving and content with ordinary things. Not someone always reaching, always driving, always pushing. She needed a man . . . like Dave, she thought, watching him expertly flipping burgers. He was wearing Meg's apron with *For This I Spent Four Years in College?* emblazoned across the front.

"All right gang," Dave's voice boomed through the warm afternoon, "let's get 'em while they're hot."

Kate marveled at how Meg managed to emerge from the

kitchen with a crisp salad and a platter of steaming corn at the precise moment that the hamburgers and hot dogs arrived at the table.

Like a herd of starving buffalo, the kids and Matt came running, their hands still dripping from a quick rinse under the outdoor faucet. Matt plucked a slice of cucumber from the salad, motioning the kids not to tell, at which they giggled uncontrollably.

"Everything looks and smells delicious . . . as always, Meg," he said, this time snitching a sliver of cheese.

As always? Just how often did he eat here? Piqued for no good reason, Kate nudged the salad bowl out of his reach, but not before he nabbed a plump cherry tomato.

"Is there anything you don't like?" she snapped.

"Yep. Liver and onions and sassy women. Although I seem to be developing a latent yen for the latter." He held the tomato up, inches from her frowning lips. "Care to indulge?"

Without thinking—at least, she preferred to believe it was without thinking—Kate leaned forward the short distance necessary to snap at the offering. But instead of releasing it, his fingers lingered.

He didn't move them. The pressure against her lips and the very tip of her tongue was slight, yet it rocked her all the way to her toes. She felt frozen in this simple act that had suddenly become very sensuous, while all around them kids spilled ketchup and argued over who got the biggest pickle. Matt was feeling it, too, she realized, watching a look of wonder slowly filter into his eyes.

At last he dropped his hand, relinquishing the tomato and, along with it, his mesmerizing hold on her, and said softly, "Enjoy."

Enjoy? Kate seriously doubted she would even be able to swallow. Her mouth and throat were bone dry, making her grateful for the spirit of confusion at her sister's table, which permitted her sudden loss of appetite to pass unnoticed.

It was nerves, she assured herself. Just nerves. All the last-minute work before she could leave the shop in California, worry over the new shop here, and then, on top of all that, to be saddled with Matt. Temporarily saddled. Tomorrow at least that problem would be behind her.

Out of the corner of her eye she saw Matt digging into his second hamburger. Worry over finding other accommodations obviously wasn't affecting his appetite. Was he really foolish . . . or arrogant . . . enough to believe he could bring her around in one day?

"Did you finally get that generator going?" Dave asked him between bites.

"Yes and no," replied Matt. "We managed to get it working temporarily, but I had to pull another electrician off a job on the mainland to come over and do the job right. It's all squared away now."

"Do you think you'll open on target?"

Matt finished chugging a mouthful of beer. "It looks like it. I've arranged for an island realtor, Mike Ferri, to handle advertising and sales on this end. He's already started co-ordinating plans for the grand opening."

"He's a good man," Dave said, nodding approvingly, "and I think giving the business to a native will go a long way toward winning you public support."

"That's what I'm counting on," agreed Matt.

Kate listened in growing disbelief as both Meg and Dave deluged Matt with tips on how to make the condominiums more palatable to their fellow year-round residents. When Meg came up with the bright idea of opening the planned child-care center to all residents, Kate couldn't keep quiet any longer.

"This is incredible. I thought you two were such gung-ho environmentalists—you know, preserve island rusticity at all costs. Since when do you put the interests of some outsider"—she fairly sneered the word—"ahead of the good of the local community?"

The kids had long since finished their hot dogs and been excused. Now the adults stopped eating, and an awkward silence enveloped the table. Meg and Dave seemed almost embarrassed by her outburst.

Matt regarded her calmly, apparently unperturbed at being called an outsider. "My project is good for the local community. It will mean more jobs and a wider tax base and, most important, a new source of income for the local economy."

"Not to mention a new source of income for Kincade Construction," she added spitefully.

Matt's eyes were serious, not a bit guilty. "That, too."

He picked up his corn and nonchalantly munched away, completely unaffected by her attack. Watching him, Kate bristled anew at his smug attitude.

"You really enjoy forcing your will on people, don't you?"

"Only when I know it's in their best interests."

Their eyes locked across the table, hers accusing, his challenging, both of them aware that they were talking about much more than condominiums.

"Whew." Dave's low whistle broke the ice . . . barely. "And I thought this was going to be just another long, dull summer. Things should be pretty interesting with you two living under the same roof. Maybe I could pick up a little extra cash selling ringside seats."

It was Kate's turn to look smug. "I wouldn't count on it, Dave. Matt won't be living in the lighthouse much longer. As a matter of fact, he'll be moving out first thing in the morning." She turned to watch his face as she twisted the knife. "Isn't that right, Matt?"

"Actually, it's absolutely wrong." He turned his attention to an intrigued Dave and a concerned-looking Meg. "The fact of the matter is that Kate and I will continue to share the lighthouse—in a spirit of mutual cooperation—until I finish my work here."

Kate felt strangely betrayed. For all his annoying tendencies, she hadn't expected Matt to break his word to her.

"But you said—"

"I said," he cut in, "that I would leave in the morning if you still wanted me to."

"I do. And believe me, I'll still want you to in the morning."

"No, you won't. Not if it means losing the lease on the shop you're planning to rent in Old Harbor. You said yourself that rentals get mighty scarce this close to Memorial Day. Why, I'll bet you won't be able to find another place available anywhere near the tourist district."

A tight ball of nerves began to form in the pit of Kate's stomach, making her thankful she hadn't eaten more than a few bites. "What does your staying or going have to do with my renting that shop?"

Matt slapped his palm against his forehead in a spirit of comical exaggeration that was wasted on Kate at the moment. "Did I forget to mention that little detail? I told you my Uncle Chester left me the land I'm building the condominiums on, didn't I? Well, he also left me a piece of commercial property right in the middle of Old Harbor."

Kate's eyelids lowered. "Oh no."

"Oh yes." Her eyes opened in time to see Matt's dark brown mustache curl above a supremely triumphant grin. "Thanks to good old Uncle Chester, I own the building where your shop will be located. Or should I say, where your shop would have been located?"

Kate thought of the spacious, airy shop located on a pretty, flower-bordered cul-de-sac, and her heart dropped to her heels. "You'd really refuse to rent the shop to me if I don't agree to let you go on living in the lighthouse?"

He shrugged, a gesture that was becoming irritatingly familiar to Kate. "It seems only fair."

Meg's gaze volleyed between Matt's smiling face and Kate's stricken one. "Matt, I think you're being—"

"I think," interrupted Dave, "that this is none of our business. Come on, I'll help you with the dishes."

"We used paper plates," Meg reminded him.

"Then I'll help you throw them away." He gave her a pointed look.

Getting to his feet along with them, Matt said, "That's all right, Dave. If you two will forgive us for eating and running, I think Kate and I will be leaving. I have a hunch we have a lot to talk about."

Kate could see Meg biting her lip to keep out of it, and she was grateful. Having all her well-laid plans jerked out from under her left her feeling not quite up to a communal discussion.

She quickly said good-bye to the kids, her spirits buoyed slightly by the wet, noisy kiss Brian willingly planted somewhere in the general vicinity of her cheek, and climbed into Matt's truck.

About halfway home, he tapped her on the shoulder and asked, "Should I interpret your silence as acquiescence?"

"Only if you're crazier than I thought," Kate snapped.

After that, silence reigned once more. As soon as they entered the lighthouse, Kate bolted for the stairs, deciding to postpone the surrender she knew was inevitable for as long as possible.

"Kate."

The word—actually more of a command—told Kate he was only a step behind her. Having no doubt he would have the temerity to trail her right into her bedroom, she stopped dead in her tracks, causing him to do the same.

His hands jerked upward, grasping her arms above the elbow; the action, at first reflex, soon turned provocative. His body was pressed against her back as he brought his lips close to her ear. She picked up a clean drift of fragrance that was nearly as devastating to her senses as the soothing movements of his fingers.

"You really ought to signal when you're going to stop short," he whispered. "But then, who'd have dreamed a rear-end collision could be such heady stuff?"

Break away: The message carried from her brain on a wave of adrenaline was delivered to limbs as steady as marshmallow fluff.

"Is the prospect of being my roommate really so horrible?" he asked quietly.

Kate broke his light hold and whirled to face him. "Yes. Especially when I'm being blackmailed into it."

"I think the term *blackmail* is a little dramatic, don't you, Kate? I prefer to think of this as a textbook example of creative bargaining."

Kate's look could have frozen a lake in July. "I always thought the term *barter* applied only when both parties involved are willing to trade, and in case you haven't noticed, I am not willing."

"Of course you are. Face it, Kate, I have something you want, namely the lease on the shop, and you have something I want." He paused long enough to slide his gaze over her in an intimate manner that was also becoming far too familiar for Kate's liking. "More than one thing that I want, actually, but for now let's limit our negotiations to the lighthouse."

Kate stared up into his face. At thirty-two, it was already weathered and lined and experienced beyond any description as meek as "handsome." As he stared back, waiting, tiny crinkle lines deepened around his eyes, suggesting a natural wariness and the instincts of a born survivor. He wasn't about to back down.

Wishing she was heartless enough to shove him over the banister, she said, "I'd love to tell you what you can do with your stinking lease."

"But you're not that pig-headed," he returned, a not-so-subtle emphasis on the word *that*. "You want this new shop to succeed so badly you can taste it, and I know what that tastes like. You're not about to let anger get in the way of all that."

The miserable part of the whole thing was that he was right. Now all that remained were the formalities. But, if Matt Kincade expected any fringe benefits from this little coup, he was in for a surprise—not to mention a whole lot of frustration. Forcing a smile, Kate prepared to make the most limited surrender in history.

"You're right, Matt. I accept your terms."

Inside, all her senses were racing, sending the crucial messages to unclench fists and stop biting lip to the appropriate body parts. But on the surface she was the epitome of cool control, her manner properly docile, her smile a study in sincerity.

The 360-degree reversal in attitude wiped the self-satisfied grin right off Matt's face. His eyes narrowed suspiciously.

"Why? I mean, what made you change your mind all of a sudden?"

"I thought this is what you wanted." Her look of wide-eyed innocence, intended to confuse him further, was an unqualified success.

"It was what I wanted. What I want now is to know what's behind this sudden about-face."

"You've simply convinced me of the wisdom of your reasoning. As you pointed out, it's a perfect example of creative bargaining, pure and simple."

"If it's so pure and simple, why do I have the distinct feeling there's a catch in it somewhere?" he grumbled.

Kate shrugged, a reassuring smile on her lips. "I guess you're just naturally suspicious. Don't worry, it's common among us ambitious types."

"Then, just to satisfy my nasty suspicious streak, why don't you tell me exactly what I'll be getting in exchange for the lease on the shop."

"The lease on the lighthouse, of course."

He caught her hand, foiling her attempt to take the few steps into her room. "And?"

He was asking for it. Had, in fact, been asking for it since they'd met. A more calculating businesswoman might have been able to resist the temptation to let him have it. Kate couldn't.

"And nothing," she said slowly, distinctly, as if he might miss the message. "Our relationship will be that of two professionals. The fact that we happen to be living under the same roof will in no way affect the nature of that relationship. There will be no morning coffee klatches, no sharing laundry detergent, no palsy-walsy little dinners. And I will take great pains to preserve this distance between us."

Kate heaved a deep sigh, a little amazed at her own vehemence. Thrusting her chin out defiantly, she stared into Matt's eyes. At this moment they were completely devoid of all emotion, and that made them all the more menacing.

"I see," he nodded, exhibiting no anger, no disappointment, no emotion whatsoever. "In other words, you're proposing a sort of peaceful but unfriendly coexistence?"

It was Kate's turn to nod. It occurred to her that Matt might welcome this sort of arrangement once he had a chance to think about it. Some men felt obliged to come on to every woman they encountered, and this up-front, point-blank rejection might simplify life for both of them. She began to feel the first faint stirrings of relief.

"Once the shop lease is signed," he continued in the same unemotional monotone, "we will be committed to a strictly professional relationship, no friendly propositions, no personal overtures. Do I have it straight?"

Kate nodded eagerly. He was going to go along with it.

"In that case . . ."

Moving quickly and resolutely against her, he trapped Kate between the solid wall of the hallway and the almost equally solid wall of his tautly held body. He cradled her chin in one strong hand and used the rough, sunbrowned fingers of the other to stroke a feathery gold curl back from her cheek. His face was so close Kate could feel his breath heating her skin, and when he whispered, she felt and saw the words as well as heard them.

"Lady, I've been aching to do this all day, and I damn well wouldn't want to be guilty of breaking our lease."

Her automatic protest was muffled against Matt's lips as they claimed hers, slowly and with consummate tenderness. He made no effort to intrude past the vulnerable barrier they presented, seemingly content to savor the experience of tasting her with his own moist and slightly open mouth. It was one of the gentlest kisses she'd ever experienced, and, Kate realized, one of the most seductive.

Briefly, she contemplated the merits of struggling and vetoed the idea. On a purely physical level, Matt held an undeniable advantage. Besides, maybe the best way to drive home the message that she was not interested was to let him take his best shot, and then squelch him by emerging completely unaffected. That plan had the added advantage of putting him on the receiving end of a little smug condescension for a change.

Predictably, the kiss soon escalated from exploratory to insistent, with his tongue and teeth coaxing her lips to part with the same self-confident purposefulness Kate suspected he brought to every new challenge. Poor man, he had no way of knowing that her years of experience observing this kind of single-minded male approach made her eminently qualified to resist it.

But when Matt abandoned his attempt to deepen the kiss, and instead strewed tiny, nibbling kisses along her jaw to an especially susceptible spot on the side of her throat, Kate realized that remaining unaffected was not going to be the excerise in simplicity she'd anticipated. The rough texture of his mustache and the softness of his lips were creating a duet of exquisitely pleasurable sensations.

It had been over a year since she'd left Jeff, and even longer since they'd shared anything more intimate than a joint checking account. She blamed her long fast for the sudden outrageous urge to yield to Matt all the abandoned responses he came closer to unleashing with each brushstroke of his lips.

With slow, firm pressure, he slid his hands over her shoulders, tracing the line of her spine with his fingertips, ending by cupping the rounded curve of her hips. En route he managed to mold every inch of her wavering body to his. The shivers of excitement that had been dancing along her nerve endings suddenly fused into a fiery whirlpool of longing deep in the pit of her stomach. Without registering the subtle degrees of change, Kate slipped from the conscious resolve not to resist, to not wanting to resist, to the point of not being able to break the bonds of desire she had allowed Matt to forge.

Totally relinquishing the role of passive participant, she let her hands explore the hard surface of his back, roaming up the warm column of his neck to bury themselves in the thick waves of hair just above his collar. Her cooperation seemed to spur Matt on. He inched his hands down until his fingers curved into her rounded bottom, causing Kate to catch her breath as he brought their bodies into even more intimate contact.

This time when his lips wandered to feather light kisses along her cheek and in the sensitive hollow behind her ear, Kate awaited their return with an eagerness that bordered on desperation. When his mouth moved hungrily to hers, she willingly succumbed to the pleasantly abrasive exploration of his tongue, returning the pleasure with slow, deep strokes of her own. It seemed only natural when his hands lifted to her breasts, making them tingle and tighten with the slow, intoxicating movements of his fingers. For a time that seemed all too short, they clung to each other, refining the art of touching and being touched, discovering and being discovered.

Then, as languorously and deliberately as he had lured her in, Matt began to lead her out of the intricate labyrinth of passion they had created together. He withdrew the pleasing warmth of his tongue with minuscule circular strokes that enticed even as they soothed, until with only the barest pressure his lips traced hers in a lingering kiss. Kate felt his hands slip from her breasts, and along with it, the awkward return of reason.

Had she really believed she could withstand the temptation of his kiss? After last night? After today, when even his casual touches had sizzled against her skin? It was a slight consolation, but the only one available, to note that

Matt seemed to be having equal difficulty shifting his breathing back into low gear. It wasn't enough to lessen her discomfort or improve her self-esteem at that moment.

"It looks like we're going to have to renegotiate that lease, darlin'," he said more softly than she'd imagined he could speak. "Shall we go up to my room and work on it?"

Kate winced inwardly. Of course it was foolish to hope Matt might proceed with gentlemanly discretion. At least when she pushed against him, he made no effort to hold her.

"Absolutely not. This little lapse into adolescent behavior doesn't alter our situation one iota. I still have no desire for any personal contact with you whatsoever." She took a step into her room, then swung around to add, "And I hope you'll keep that in mind in the future."

"Yes, ma'am. I'll be sure to keep it in mind." A smile spread slowly across his face, lifting his mustache in a way that matched the wicked gleam in his dark eyes. "As a matter of fact, I plan to make satisfying your desires the focal point of all my attention in the coming weeks."

4

THROUGH SOME CRAFTY evasive maneuvers, Kate managed to avoid coming face to face with Matt for the next few days. Still, he haunted her. Her days began with a sunrise serenade as he belted out a rousing chorus of "Oh, What a Beautiful Morning" from the bathroom across the hall, displaying an impressive amount of vigor for a man who rolled in at close to midnight each night. The fact that she lay awake, aware of the exact moment he came home, irritated Kate nearly as much as her growing curiosity about what—or who—occupied his long evenings.

But if Matt's body was absent from the lighthouse for most of the day, his spirit was annoyingly present, and by Wednesday morning Kate was convinced he was waging a one-man crusade to disprove the old platitude "out of sight; out of mind." She stepped into the bathroom and was assailed by the scent of him. Not some fancy cologne or after shave . . . just him. It was a blending of fresh smells—his soap, his shampoo, the lime shaving foam he used—and it seemed to linger in her head the rest of the day.

Then there were the messages, a new one each morning, slathered across the bathroom mirror in white shaving foam. Annoyingly provocative though they were, she had to admit he was developing a real flair with an aerosal can.

She raised a washcloth to wipe the latest away, then flung it back down. Maybe if he had to clean up his own mess for a change, he'd tire of the whole childish game. Less subtle messages of discouragement certainly weren't doing much good, she realized, peering into the new wicker hamper she'd bought for her own personal use. The homey sight of his jeans nestled snugly amongst her lacy lingerie brought all Kate's resentment bubbling to the surface, calling forth a spiteful streak she hadn't known she possessed. If it was laundry service he wanted, then that's what he would get.

Seething with righteous indignation, she dragged the hamper down to the kitchen and, stopping only long enough to pluck out her own light-colored items, heaved the rest into the washer, flipped the temperature control to hot, and slammed the lid closed with her first smile of the morning. Nothing like a nice long soak with a red jersey to give a man's briefs a dash of color. Later, transferring the clean wash to the dryer, she held up a pair of his cotton briefs, now an enchanting shade of pink, and thought perhaps she should feel a twinge of guilt. She didn't. She felt satisfied. Nasty, but satisfied nonetheless.

Unfortunately, the feeling was fleeting. An hour later, unpacking quilting supplies in the back room of the still very disorganized shop, she faced the fact that Matt Kincade had her at his mercy—again—and he didn't even know it yet.

"You're going to have to ask him sooner or later," Meg said, reading her mind. "Preferably sooner. These quilts have to be hung, and you can't go drilling holes in a brick wall without asking the landlord first."

Kate interrupted her count of pattern books to glare at her sister. "I thought you stopped by to help. Sitting there lecturing me on what I already know is not helping."

"Well, if you already know it, why don't you do something about it?"

Her gaze dropped back to the patterns. "I'm going to."

"When?"

"Soon."

"Today?"

"Maybe." Even to Kate the reply sounded wishy-washy.

"Kate," Meg began in her best big sister voice.

"How can I ask him when I never even see him?" interrupted Kate.

"You live in the same house, for pete's sake."

"Yeah, but he leaves before I get up and comes home after I'm in bed."

The idea of anyone working so hard brought forth all Meg's motherly concern. "Poor Matt. I knew this project had him working long hours, but that's ridiculous."

"Poor Matt, my eye," Kate snapped with a vengeance that was in itself very revealing. "I'll give you ten to one it's not work that's keeping him up nights."

Meg smiled and said not a word.

"You know I'm probably right," Kate rolled on. "Matt Kincade hardly seems the type to go for long without female companionship."

Meg just smiled.

"And even if he is working all those hours, it just proves what I already said about his being obsessed with financial success."

"Like Jeff?" asked Meg with raised eyebrows.

"You're damned right like Jeff!" Kate shouted, then wondered why she was shouting at Meg.

Her sister's eyebrows arched higher. "None of which alters the fact that you could drive out to the site and ask him and have the whole thing over with right now."

"Now?" Kate couldn't have sounded more horrified if she'd just been told she had only an hour to live. She looked around the shop furtively. "I can't. All this unpacking . . ."

"Is in expert hands. Dave doesn't expect me back for at least an hour."

Meg lifted Kate's purse from a nearby counter, hooked it over her sister's shoulder, and propelled her, still mumbling half-baked excuses, out the door.

Kate was still mumbling as she drove through the quaint streets of the shopping district, bypassing Corn Neck Road, the direct route to the northern tip of the island, in favor of the more scenic—and slower—coast road.

It was annoying, not to mention humiliating, to have to go begging a favor from Matt after her dramatic little speech about keeping things strictly business between them. Of course, her mission today was all business, but she had a strong suspicion Matt would tease and twist until it seemed something entirely different.

She sighed and drove a little slower. No doubt about it, she was at his mercy—a dangerously uncomfortable place to be, considering the man's tendency to behave like a modern-day Merchant of Venice . . . and her suspicions about which pound of her flesh interested him most. At least he hadn't seen the clean laundry yet.

She took a right by a small sign bearing the same logo as the side of Matt's truck and stopped about a hundred yards down the rough-paved road, where redwood-shingled town houses were being built in a semicircle, following the natural slope of the terrain down to the sea. With one glance, Kate understood why Matt had chosen the name Seaside Arboretum. Except for the area close to the town houses, the heavily wooded land had been left untouched. Tall maples and a seemingly endless variety of pines curtained the site on three sides, with the Atlantic forming the final border.

She scanned the busy work area, growing steadily more apprehensive. It hadn't occurred to her that she might have to go looking for Matt; she'd just assumed there would be an office of some sort. But the closest thing to an official-looking building in sight was the trailer parked off to her left. The area was crawling with construction workers, and belatedly she realized that her cut-off denims and light-blue jersey that didn't rate a second glance in town were not such a common sight around here.

She was still debating whether to start her search at the trailer or approach the small group of men standing with their backs to her, when the tallest of the three removed his hard hat to wipe his brow and Kate knew she wouldn't have to go looking after all. If she hadn't been distracted, she would have picked him out right away. Something in his stance, the way he held himself erect yet with a certain carelessness, indicated an abundance of confidence and leashed energy that even from this distance was unmistakable. And, under the circumstances, a little intimidating.

At first Kate wasn't sure if she was imagining the hush that seemed to descend on the site as she stepped from the car and started her trek across the rocky stretch of ground toward Matt. But even in her worst nightmares she could never have imagined what followed. It seemed to start as a low roar that came at her from all directions, growing and splintering into a wild chorus of whistles and shouted remarks. Mercifully, the words themselves were mostly a blur. Those she could make out fell into the category of crude but complimentary, firing a red-hot flush that spread to cover every inch of her body.

Propelling herself forward through sheer will, she saw Matt straight ahead, the relative familiarity of him like a beacon in this nightmare of sound. A series of reactions flickered across the hard planes of his face: shock, then anger, which finally gave way to annoyance and a sort of grim determination.

She saw him raise one hand in the general direction of the shouts. Gradually, miraculously, the humiliating greeting tapered off, and the more normal sounds of hammer and saw resumed. Matt remained where he was, arms folded across his chest, but the men on either side of him stepped forward eagerly as Kate drew near.

The younger of the two spoke first. "I'm the foreman here, miss. Gus Barrett. Can I help you with something?"

"I think that as personnel supervisor I should be the one to help the lady," interjected the second man, extending his hand to her. "Douglas Racine, at your service."

Before Kate had a chance to reply or accept the proffered hand, Matt was at her side, the grim set of his features tempered slightly now by traces of amusement.

"It's reassuring to see that you men take your responsibilities so seriously, but the lady doesn't need any help. She belongs to me."

His voice was warm and rough and blatantly possessive, as was the arm he curled about her waist. Ordinarily, Kate would have denied his claim vehemently, but at the moment she was temporarily beyond feeling anything but gratitude. She listened as he issued a few instructions, and then he was leading her away, the approving murmurs of the two men faint but discernible behind them.

She had surmised correctly; the trailer did serve as Matt's office. It was clean, if a little spartan, with a desk, chair, cot, and small refrigerator comprising its entire contents.

Slamming the door behind them, Matt pushed Kate into the chair and stood glaring down at her. Instinctively, Kate registered how his dominant position affected the dynamics of the situation, placing her at a subtle psychological disadvantage.

"What the hell were you thinking of, showing up out here dressed—or maybe I should say undressed—like that?"

He gestured at her clothing with such stark disapproval, Kate had a crazy urge to glance down and see if there was a scarlet letter pinned to her chest.

"Probably the same thing you were thinking when you lied to those men. I am not yours."

"Maybe not . . ."

"There's no maybe about it."

"Maybe not," he repeated a little louder, "but those men out there have spent the better part of their time for the last twelve weeks here on this island, most of them without female companionship. Would you have preferred I announce you were up for grabs?"

His eyes, darkened to the color of stormy seas, didn't miss Kate's grimace as it dawned on her how much aggravation Matt's protection had spared her in this male-dominated arena.

"No." She bit her bottom lip, feeling properly sheepish. "Maybe I should be thanking you instead of arguing with you."

"It would be a welcome change," he agreed. "What can I do for you?" His expression softened to a teasing smile. "Or were you suddenly overcome with curiosity about how I spend my days?"

Kate felt a guilty flush starting. Actually, she was much more curious about how he spent his nights, but she wasn't about to admit it.

"Hardly," she replied stiffly. "I came to ask your permission to install some dowels on the brick wall at the rear of the shop. It will entail drilling holes to mount the brackets."

Matt braced himself against the corner of the gray steel desk, looking quite intrigued by her request. "Can I ask why you want to do this?"

Kate nodded briskly; her spiel was well rehearsed. "Of course. I want to use the dowels to hang quilts. That way they can be easily seen by customers, and if someone expresses interest in a particular quilt, it will be a simple matter for me to take it down and spread it out for a closer inspection." She leaned forward, caught up, as always, in enthusiasm for her work. "The quilts are so beautiful they practically sell themselves once people are able to examine the intricate workmanship up close. This method of displaying them worked very well in my other shop."

"Other shop?" His eyes widened slightly in surprise.

"I opened my first quilt shop while I was living in California."

Matt nodded. "In Santa Barbara."

"Santa Monica," she corrected.

His dark brows lifted a fraction of an inch. "There's a difference? I always thought there was a certain homogenous quality to cities west of the Mississippi."

"It sounds like you could use a crash course in geography."

His smile was playful, and magical, reaching out to her across the small space between them. "Are you making me an offer?"

How could she answer a question like that without entangling herself further or blowing her chance at getting those dowels installed?

He spared her from finding out when he said, "Tell me more about your shop."

"There isn't much to tell. I learned whatever I know about merchandising the hard way. Luckily, I'm a fast learner, and what started out as a big gamble turned into a pretty profitable business . . . and one that I happen to love. That success is what gave me the confidence to try my luck back home. I'm hoping to foster enough local interest in quilting to organize workshops. With that and the income from summer sales, I just may be one of the fortunate few who can afford to live on the island year-round."

The warm smile starting beneath the fullness of Matt's mustache was encouraging. He hadn't been that difficult to deal with after all. Of course, he hadn't exactly said yes yet, either.

"I don't think you'll have much trouble drumming up interest," he told her. "I almost feel inspired to give it a try myself. And in answer to your request, yes, by all means hang your quilts however you wish."

Kate felt her lips forming a silly, relieved grin. She couldn't believe he had been so easy on her; she should have come days ago.

"Is that all?" he asked.

"Yes . . . I mean, no." Belatedly, Kate remembered she had two other small requests. "I also wanted to ask if you might have the dowels and brackets I'll need on hand. If I order them from a hardware store on the mainland, there's no telling when they'll get here." She shrugged a little sheepishly. "The unavailability of almost everything except the bare necessities is one of the annoying little facts of island life that I conveniently forgot in my enthusiasm about coming home."

Matt nodded. "I guess there is something to be said for civilization."

"It does have its advantages," she agreed, "but then, so does having a landlord in the construction business."

Kate was struck by how much she enjoyed the pleasantly masculine sound of his chuckle.

"Spoken like a true businesswoman. I'm sure I can rummage up what you need around here somewhere."

"I don't want to leave you short on supplies."

"You won't be. I'll simply reorder whatever materials I give to you."

"Sell to me," Kate corrected. "In fact, I'd like to pay you for them up front."

Matt caught the arm that reached for her purse. "Later. I don't even know what it will cost. I'll have a bill sent to you if you insist."

"I insist," she replied firmly. Somewhere inside her the voice of reason was coaching her to keep things strictly business, but the dissident nerves in her arm and all down her spine were reacting with rebellious pleasure to the gentle kneading action of his fingers. "There's just one more little thing," she managed to get out a little shakily.

Matt smiled, not missing either the tiny quiver in her voice or the tiny goose bumps he was raising along her skin.

"I'd like you to recommend one of your men—a carpenter—I could hire to do the work for me." The words tumbled out in a rush.

Matt squinted his eyes suspiciously. "Are you going to ask me next if I'll make the quilts as well? Because I've got to tell you, I don't feel all *that* inspired."

"No. This is my last request, I swear."

"In that case, the supplies and the manpower will be on your doorstep first thing in the morning."

Kate couldn't believe she'd won all three points without any concessions or even any real aggravation. In fact, the meeting had almost been fun.

"Just like that?" she asked cautiously.

The look of feigned innocence that settled on his face at the question was not what she would call reassuring. "Why, Kate, you sound skeptical. What did you expect?"

"Oh, a little friendly blackmail. Maybe some creative bargaining thrown in for good measure," she drawled without a hint of subtlety.

"You see how sorely you've misjudged my character?" He laughed. "I'm really a very helpful, obliging sort of guy."

"Let's just say you may not be quite the ogre you appeared to be at first," she conceded.

Matt seemed inordinately pleased by the backhanded compliment. "You can't say I'm not making progress."

Kate rose nimbly to her feet, gracefully disengaging his hold on her arm in the process. "I guess that's it then," she began in a cheerful preamble to her farewell.

Matt's long legs quickly stretched out before him, forming an effective barrier to her escape. "Not quite."

The roughly drawled words shouldn't have come as a surprise, but they did. Kate sank back into the chair. She should have known he wouldn't acquiesce so easily—or so cheaply. He'd been toying with her, setting her up for the fall, and like an idiot she'd played right into his hands.

"All right, let's have it," she demanded bitterly.

"Have what?"

His nonchalant attitude snapped the suddenly tenuous threads of her patience. "The catch. That's the usual procedure, isn't it? I make a perfectly reasonable request, and you respond with some underhanded ultimatum."

"I think you have our roles confused," he remarked, his tone dry. "But at any rate, I have no intention of posing an ultimatum, just a simple question."

Kate's instinctive wariness deepened as she waited to hear the question, certain there would be nothing simple about it.

"Why did you make a special trip out here to ask me this when you could have accomplished the same thing by getting out of bed a few minutes earlier any morning this week?"

"I think the answer to that is getting a little redundant. This request, like all matters between us, is strictly business and should be handled as such. Now if you don't mind, I'd like to leave."

Matt's hand on her shoulder held her in the chair. "Ah, but I do mind. There's something else I want to know." The near-violet eyes locking on hers were searching and so intense Kate wondered if it was possible for him to will a response out of her. "Why are you afraid of me, Kate?"

Feeling cornered, and furious because of it, she snapped, "At the risk of damaging your fragile male ego, I am not afraid of you. I am simply not interested."

"It would take me about two minutes and a little decisive action to disprove that," he said with a wicked chuckle. "But pretending that it's true, are you not interested in men as a species or just this particular man?"

"Let's just say I'm not interested in a particular type of man."

"My type?"

Her silence was affirmative enough.

"I take it you have a thorough knowledge of my type on which to base this policy," he said, his tone droll.

"Very thorough. I've had years of experience observing a prime specimen at very close range."

Her answer prompted a bitter twist of a smile from Matt. "Ah, the ex-husband," he pronounced. "May I ask just what it is about me that earns me the dubious honor of being classified as the same type as your ex?"

Kate didn't need to waste time mulling over her answer, ticking off his shortcomings with an ease born of familiarity. "You're aggressive, you're hard-driving, and you're hell-bent on succeeding at any cost."

He chuckled with disbelief. "And here I thought those

were my most noble qualities. Why do they suddenly sound like unpardonable sins?"

She gave a careless shrug. "I guess it's all in the eye of the beholder."

"And all these years I thought women liked the strong, aggressive type." He reached down and wrapped his fingers around her slender wrist. "Are you telling me I'd have a better chance with you if I were a submissive failure?"

Kate had to fight not to smile at the idea of him being even remotely submissive. "Not exactly. I simply don't like being approached as if I'm something to be conquered, like a mountain or a bad habit."

The corners of his mouth lifted at that, but the eyes holding hers were serious still. "Was that your husband's approach?" he asked as if he had every right to do so.

"Not that it's any of your business, yes, it was. Jeff went after everything he wanted with the same singleminded determination. At twenty-three I may have been naive enough to find that sort of masculine aggressiveness attractive, but not now."

"I see. You're so much wiser at . . ."

"Twenty-eight," she finished for him. "And yes, I'm much wiser now." She held his gaze only for a moment, and when she spoke again, her tone was much lighter and easier than she was feeling. "And that's why you're wasting your time with me."

"I don't think time spent with you could ever be considered wasted," he said softly.

A tiny current of electricity seemed to trail his hands as they climbed her bare arms to rest securely on her shoulders. The contact was comforting, a commodity that had been in short supply in Kate's life lately, and it was tempting to just let herself melt into his strength. With his hands at the sides of her neck, he used this thumbs to tilt her chin up until his eyes, looking neither predatory nor amused now, found hers.

"Maybe your ex-husband and I have some qualities in common, Kate, but with one crucial difference; I would never be stupid enough to let you get away." He stilled her protest by gently covering her lips with rough, callused fingertips. "Give me a chance, a chance to prove I can make you happy in all the ways he failed." The corners of his mouth curved into a teasing smile. "Hell, woman, I work hard all day; I don't want to climb mountains when I get home at night."

Beneath the self-confidence burning in his bright eyes, Kate read a promise, unwavering and very unsettling, and she felt a stab of pure longing. Simultaneously she forced herself to remember that she knew better than to trust such masculine promises, particularly when they were delivered with such blatant self-assurance.

She wanted to remain aloof, or at least keep up the appearance of being so, but he was pulling responses from her that she didn't want to give. As if reading the mixture of panic and nervous confusion on her face, he didn't press any further. With a silent tenderness she hadn't expected, he ushered her outside.

The effect of the sunlight was instantaneous, chasing away the shadowy sensuality that had held them captive inside the trailer and bringing Kate fully back to her senses. She peered up at Matt after he'd helped her into the car and swung the door shut. "Matt, our talk back there . . . it doesn't change anything. I want you to understand—"

"I do understand," he interrupted with a smile. It wasn't the teasing curl of his lips he gave so easily, but a full, devastating smile that made her breath catch in her throat and left her wondering just what he thought he understood. Then, leaning closer, he muttered, "I know you'll want to make this totally convincing."

Darting a glance in the direction of the men working, he bent his head and moved his lips with unhurried enjoyment over hers. The kiss was unabashedly possessive and very convincing—even to Kate. When he lifted his head, his fingers lingered, continuing their sensuous massage of her neck. Over one of his broad shoulders Kate saw the foreman she'd met earlier, waiting, clipboard in hand.

"Drive slowly, darlin'," Matt cautioned, straightening and stepping back. "I'll see you when I get home tonight."

At the cozy farewell, a knowing grin erupted on the foreman's face.

Kate, with a facsimile of a smile frozen in place, glared at Matt's supremely triumphant grin and ground out for his ears only, "Not if I see you first, darling."

5

KATE WAS ASLEEP before Matt came home that night, and up and gone before he was even out of bed the next morning.

After a quick stop for donuts, she hustled to the shop to fix a pot of coffee before the carpenter arrived. It was already warm out, too warm for May on the island and too warm to spend the day inside working. But with the start of the tourist season only two weeks away, Kate had no choice. She plugged in the drip coffeemaker and set out some paper cups, thinking that by midmorning she'd probably be running to the diner down the street for cold drinks to keep the poor guy from dehydrating.

But a half hour later, when the carpenter came whistling through the door, clad in faded jeans and a Boston Red Sox T-shirt, lugging a tool box in one hand and a Styrofoam cooler in the other, it was not some "poor guy" from Matt's crew as she expected. It was Matt, as she should have expected.

"You were supposed to send a man." It was part complaint, part accusation, delivered to his back as he lowered the cooler to the floor.

Turning with an ironic expression, he glanced down at his torso, then up at her. "In case you haven't noticed, I fit that description."

"I meant you were supposed to send a carpenter."

"I'm that, too." He started pulling tools from the box.

"You did this on purpose."

"Of course."

She watched as he examined the brick wall, scratching experimentally at the mortar between the bricks. There wasn't much she could do about it now, even if she wanted to, which she wasn't quite sure she did.

"Do you want a cup of coffee?"

He turned and smiled, looking slightly surprised by the offer but obviously pleased. "Sure. With extra cream, and a jelly donut, please." Nodding at the box of assorted donuts, he added, "You sure know how to ensure good service."

Kate handed him the coffee and donut along with a paper napkin. "Just a little trick I picked up from my mother. And she seems to be something of an expert on pleasing men, judging by the way her books sell."

"I think it's great, her being a writer and all. She's a terrific lady."

"Yeah, she is pretty terrific," Kate agreed with a laugh, thinking of her spitfire mother dragging her dad halfway around the globe under the pretext of serious research.

"Do you read them?" Matt asked between bites.

"Her books? Of course I read them. What's that look for?"

"Nothing. It's just that I got the impression you were opposed to romance in any way, shape, or form. I guess if it's safely contained between the pages of a book, then it's acceptable."

Exasperated, Kate swatted at the strands of tawny hair that had slipped from her barrette. "Don't start," she ordered. "Or rather, do start—on the job you're to do."

He chuckled at her discomfiture, but he obliged, fetching a stepladder from his truck when she explained how high she wanted the top brackets mounted. While he worked Kate continued unpacking and arranging and rearranging stock. At one point she paused in her search for the perfect place to display a muslin and Wedegwood-blue quilted pillow and watched him drive the final nail into the first bracket.

"I think you're going to need extra support," she offered in what she thought was a helpful manner.

"No, this will be fine."

"I don't think so," she said a bit more firmly. "These quilts may look light, but they're really pretty heavy."

This time he peered down from the top of the ladder, wiping the back of his hand across his damp brow. "I said this will be fine, and it will be."

"But in the other shop—"

"Well, this isn't the other shop," he cut in, his voice rising, "and I'm using six-penny-weight masonry nails, and it will be fine."

Kate bristled at his impatience. Six-penny-weight certainly didn't sound all that sturdy to her. "It'd better be," she hissed, itching to hurl the pillow at the broad back he once again turned to her. Instead, she whirled on the heel of one sneaker and shoved the pillow onto the first shelf she passed.

Lord, he was arrogant, she thought, feeling angry without wanting to. She didn't want to feel anger or any other emotion toward Matt. She wanted to feel blessed nothingness toward him. But it was darn hard. He could draw her to anger quicker than anyone she'd ever known, and it was unnerving. What other responses would he be able to draw from her if he managed to get close enough?

The temper that fueled her efforts seemed to have a similar effect on Matt, and for a long time the only sounds were those of Kate ripping open crates and the furious banging—punctuated with an occasional colorful oath—from the outer room. When she finished checking the shipment of craft books against the invoice, she brushed away the stray hairs clinging to the damp skin of her neck and headed out to pour herself a cup of coffee, wishing she had the nerve to ask what was in the cooler instead.

Matt was sitting on the top of the ladder, tugging off his shirt, and Kate got an eyeful of bronze shoulders and hard chest before turning back to the considerably less appetizing sight of the now muddy coffee.

"Kate." His deep voice beckoned her attention back to him again. "Will you hand me a beer from the cooler? Please."

It wasn't exactly an apology for snapping at her. She tried to regard him frostily, a formidable task considering the beseeching manner in which he was smiling down at her.

"It's only eleven o'clock in the morning," she reminded him.

"So? I get just as thirsty at eleven in the morning as I do at two in the afternoon."

That made enough sense to move her to the cooler. She fished out a slippery bottle from the assortment of soda and beer and handed it up to him before helping herself to an orange soda.

"Kate?"

"What?"

"I'm hungry, too."

"Eat another donut."

"I already did."

She glanced at the open donut box and the sprinkling of crumbs that was all that remained. "And you're still hungry?"

"I can't help it. I haven't done this much physical labor in years," he grumbled exaggeratedly. "Besides, I couldn't have any cereal this morning. Somebody forgot to buy milk."

"Not *somebody*," she corrected touchily. "You. I am not your housekeeper."

He swung down from the ladder, a slow grin beginning at one corner of his mouth as he faced her, his closeness pleasing and disturbing at the same time. "Well, it's easy to see how I could become confused. I mean, you did such a bang-up job on my laundry, I thought you'd changed your mind about handling all our domestic chores."

Kate could feel her face turning as pink as the waistband of the briefs he tugged up for her to see. "*We* don't have any domestic chores. And if you'd thrown your dirty clothes in your own hamper, that never would have happened."

He was all innocent smiles. "Do you hear me complaining? I always found basic white a little bland for my taste. I'll just have to be careful not to use the john out at the site when any of the men are around. You know, I have my image to preserve."

She took a long look at him standing there, pleased as punch, the essence of masculinity with his thumb hitched in that ridiculous hot-pink underwear, and burst out laughing. It felt good to be laughing, really laughing. Her shoulders shook as the wave of giggles rolled on, spontaneous, refreshing, somehow almost cleansing.

When it ebbed, she wiped a tear from her eye and told him in gross understatement, "You are impossible."

She wondered at the enchanted expression on his face as he smiled agreeably. "Yup. And even hungrier than I was five minutes ago. So do you go for sandwiches, or do I?"

In the end, they went for the sandwiches together, carrying them down to the ferry landing where they discovered that some seagulls like sliced pepperoni and some wouldn't touch it with a six-foot beak.

For Kate, the afternoon rolled by more easily in some respects and not so easily in others. Matt finished mounting the dowels, adding extra braces only after the first quilt they hung wrenched the six-penny-weight masonry nail right out of its mooring. He even did it cheerfully, making her laugh all over again when he grumbled, "You could have warned me about how heavy these damn things are."

Still, when she tried to suggest—oh-so-tactfully—that he fluff the quilts a bit more in the middle as he hung them, it started all over again.

"I only have two hands," he growled. "I can't puff and hang at the same time."

"Then come down, and I'll do it myself."

His foot had barely cleared the bottom rung when she was up on it.

"Boy, you sure are bossy," he commented pleasantly, steadying the ladder while she fussed with the rose-toned log-cabin quilt.

"And you sure are pig-headed," she tossed back, not quite so pleasantly.

Warm fingers teased her ankle and tiptoed up her calf. "You see? We're made for each other."

The roughly drawled words had a spine-tingling effect. His fingers climbed to mid-thigh, imparting a sweet, soft thrill with each centimeter gained until Kate was afraid her legs would buckle under her.

"Stop that." With one hand she swatted his away.

"Just trying to help."

She gazed down, catching the undercurrent of excitement in his lazy look, and said, "That's not helping."

Matt just smiled and leaned back to watch her work, looking very pleased indeed with the effect his touch had had on her. Nobly, Kate attempted to keep on working under his intent gaze, which warmed her more than the eighty-degree temperature. When she had tugged and folded and poked at the quilt for what seemed like hours and still hadn't gotten it right, she backed down the ladder, totally exasperated.

"I give up. You do it. Don't puff, don't plump, just hang them, and I'll fix it all up later." She swung around to find him grinning at her, arms folded in front of him. "Now what?"

"Nothing. I was just watching you climb down and thinking you have the most fantastic"—his eyes danced wickedly—"quilts."

He reached out and put his hands on her arms, slipping his fingers beneath the short sleeves of her cotton top.

"Don't." The soft command lacked authority.

"Don't what, Kate?"

"Don't touch me. Don't make me laugh. Don't make it any harder than it already is for me to fight you."

"Do you have to fight me?" His voice was soft now, too.

She nodded solemnly. "Yes."

"It's a losing battle, you know."

Her eyelids fluttered shut. She knew. She also knew she couldn't afford to lose and that he would never understand that, so she just remained silent. He tilted his head to the side and studied her for a long moment. Then he hugged her close, his husky laugh flowing over her like liquid silk.

"Oh, but Kate, just think of all the fun we're going to have when you finally surrender."

That brought her head up. "I won't."

"I know." He kissed her forehead, the tip of her nose, her chin. "You'll never surrender. So let's just get back to work, shall we?"

By the time he got hungry again, the quilts were all hung, the back room was cleared of empty crates, and the place was beginning to look more like a real shop than a

warehouse after a hurricane blew through. They were standing on the sidewalk, admiring all they had accomplished.

"Thank you, Matt." She smiled up at him. "You pitched
in above and beyond the call of a landlord's duty today,
and I appreciate it."

"Then you won't mind helping me out with something?"

The spirit of the afternoon spent working side by side
pitched Kate off guard. Totally unsuspecting, she replied,
"Of course not. What can I do?"

His smile turned roguish, and she knew she'd been had.

"Come help me christen the pool out at the site," he
invited.

She shouldn't. It was already dusk. A moonlit swim with
Matt did not even approach her idea of prudent behavior.
"I don't think so," she replied, immediately wishing she'd
sounded more emphatic.

"Come on. It'll feel great to cool off."

"I don't even have a suit with me." Smart, Kate, real
smart. Could you have given him a wider opening?

Mercifully, he ignored the chance to get in a cheap shot.
"You can wear what you have on. There'll be no one there
but us." When she hesitated, he leaned forward and whispered, "I'll even throw in a pizza."

Knowing she shouldn't, Kate smiled back at him and
was lost.

The mood of the site was different at night. Bathed in a
deepening violet haze, devoid of human sounds, it seemed
whimsical, almost magical. Soft night breezes carried the
spicy incense of the sea and the chirpings of countless crick-
ets.

Pleasantly full from the pizza, Kate sat on the tile edge
of the pool, dangling her legs in the cool water and feeling
glad she had come. However, the relaxed mood that enveloped her was doomed to a short life. A movement behind
and a little to her right caught her eye, and she turned to
see Matt, bare-chested in the starlight, unbuckling his belt.

"What are you doing?" she asked, displaying a hitherto
unknown ability to question the obvious.

"Taking off my jeans," he replied, doing so with long-
legged grace.

"You said we could leave our clothes on."

"Uh-uh. I said *you* could leave your clothes on. I refuse to be immortalized as the jerk who drowned while dragging around twenty pounds of wet denim." With obvious intent, he hooked his thumbs in the waistband of the snug-fitting briefs that had taken on a fluorescent quality in the glow of the moon.

Unadulterated panic welled inside her. "Wait. Those don't weigh anywhere near twenty pounds."

"No. But in the event of an accident, I don't want to be fished out wearing shocking-pink underwear, either."

She chewed her lip. "I could always promise to remove them posthumously."

"Nice try, but I don't trust you."

She swung around as his thumbs headed south and didn't look again until the hard, bronze length of him arrowed into the water beside her feet.

He swam, she decided, the way he did everything else: powerfully, with long, aggressive strokes that gobbled up the water in front of him and left it in a disturbed vortex behind. He would be the same as a lover, she was certain. Forceful, energetic, demanding as much as he gave. The vision made her blush in the darkness and sent a twist of desire ripping through her.

She was startled back to awareness by a cascade of water as Matt rose from the depths of the pool to grip the rounded ledge on either side of her.

"Hi."

"Hi." She was slightly breathless from her thoughts of a moment ago—and from new thoughts of the half of him concealed below water.

Her gaze flew to his. She was moved by the tenderness she saw there and shocked by the perception. Using a treading motion to stay afloat, he took her hands in his. A smile, slow and cunning, lifted the dark mustache shimmering with water droplets.

"You know, I think I was right that first night, when I said the sight of my nakedness got you all hot and bothered. I think what you need is"—the next words rushed past as she was hauled face first into the water on top of him—"a good cooling off."

She came up sputtering and fighting mad. "You're despicable. I don't know why I even agreed to come here with you. I knew you'd pull something like this."

"The only thing I pulled was you," he pointed out innocently, peeling wet waves of hair from her face.

She slapped away the hand he placed at her waist to buoy her up. "You know what I mean . . . swimming naked, dragging me in here . . ."

"Shhhh."

"I will not shhh," she hissed on a rising note.

"Shhhh." This time the hushing noise was accompanied by a firm finger against her lips. "We have a visitor."

Oh no. Caught swimming with a naked man—it would be all over the island come sunrise. Kate didn't even want to look, but he put his arms around her and gently turned her so her back was against his chest. At the side of the pool, sniffing the folded bundle of Matt's clothes, was a ball of black-and-white-striped fur.

"A skunk," she breathed, feeling ridiculously relieved until a new worry assailed her. "Do you think he'll spray us in here?"

Matt was so close, the day's-end stubble on his chin grated against her shoulder when he spoke. "I doubt it, but I don't relish the idea of startling him into attacking my clothes, either."

"It would serve you right," she gloated.

He bit her earlobe lightly. "If he does, I won't put them back on. How will you like being escorted home by me as I am?"

That made her bite her tongue. Finally, with a bored glance around, their guest ambled off into the woods area beyond the town houses, eliciting an audible sigh of relief from the couple frozen in the middle of the pool.

They were both treading water to stay afloat, his hair-roughened legs sweeping against hers too accurately and too often for it to be accidental. In the silky depths of the water, his light touch seemed extraordinarily intimate, stirring something deep inside her.

With a quick twisting motion, she was out of his arms, calling back over one shoulder, "As long as I'm in here, I might as well swim."

After only a few strokes, she understood Matt's point about the jeans. Her own shorts felt like a suit of soggy armor, and the short sleeves of her top were like rubber bands hindering her every move. She stuck it out for a lap and a half, then retired to the shallow end, bracing her elbows on the pool edge.

The pool surface was an unbroken mirror of shimmering black. That meant Matt was somewhere below, probably heading in her direction right now. Tiny goose bumps of anticipation erupted all over her skin, and as if on cue he emerged directly in front of her, a tantalizing half smile on his face. As he slowly narrowed the distance between them, it became an effort for Kate just to breathe. Under the hypnotic spell of his gaze, she watched, a mesmerized audience of one, as his hands reached out to pull the wet jersey tautly across her breasts. The tips were already puckered from the comparative coolness of the water, presenting him with a most provocative silhouette.

"I haven't seen your bathing suit, but I already know I like this a whole lot better." His voice was husky, pitched low, adding to her feeling that they were all alone in the world.

He drifted a step closer, not close enough so their bodies were touching, but enough to make all the fine hairs on her body stand on end. Even while a small part of her ordered retreat, Kate knew it was already too late. She was caught— or rather, captivated—by this man she'd sworn to resist. His gentle touch had simply coalesced the longings and yearnings that had been germinating within her all day into a palpable force that held her feet rooted to the pool's smooth bottom.

His hands relinquished her shirt to skitter over her arms, her shoulders, her cheeks, until just the pads of his fingers rested lightly against her temples. Then, as she watched, transfixed, he closed his eyes and proceeded to learn her face by touch alone.

In slow, will-o'-the-wisp circles and graceful curling vines, he trailed his fingers along her hairline, across her forehead, stroking each eyebrow from the center out. His touch was ephemeral as he gently closed the lids of her eyes, then finger-kissed the soft hollows beneath them. With the balls of his thumbs, he grazed her nose, discovering and lingering at the slight indentation across the bridge.

"Broken?" he inquired softly.

Kate's eyes flickered open to find his still closed, his expression tinged with curiosity.

Her words came out soft, breathy. "No. I cut it falling off a curb when I was two."

Without opening his eyes or saying a word, he planted a kiss on the spot of the hurt long healed, then continued his tactile exploration. He caressed her cheeks and sent shivers racing up her spine by lightly grazing the soft, nerve-rich skin below her ear and along the side of her neck. When he reached her lips, Kate, lost in the wonder of his touch, sighed against his fingertips.

He traced the rim of her mouth with his thumb, dipping inside to steal some of her own moisture and spread it over the suddenly dry surface. Through it all she remained still, wishing fervently that he would replace those fingers, their touch still as light as the night breeze, with his lips. But instead of kissing her, he trailed his fingers lower, and as one finger slipped inside the rounded neck of her top, she saw his strong hand tremble ever so slightly.

"Oh, Kate." Her heart lurched inside at the sound of the raspy groan deep in his throat. "You feel . . . beautiful."

Using that same one finger, he tugged the neck of her shirt into a deep V, until she could feel the night air cooling her skin. At last he opened his eyes. For a long, intense moment he just gazed at her. His face, lit by moonglow, appeared open, guileless, holding an appeal she couldn't resist, didn't want to resist.

His lips parted slightly as he bent his head, and then his tongue, hot and moist, bathed the soft upper swell of her breast, making the flames burning in the pit of her stomach flare higher.

"You taste beautiful, too," he whispered against her skin as his other hand brushed low along her spine. With the mildest of pressure he drew her closer until his thighs were molded to hers and his hardness lay cushioned against her stomach.

He was wooing her, Kate realized dreamily, with finesse, with tenderness and expertise, but without even a suggestion of force. But for Kate, his careful restraint had become exquisite torture; the flame had become an ache. Unconsciously her fingers had been kneading his shoulders; now she wove them into the tangled dampness of his hair and brought his head up.

Trembling with the force of her growing desire, her eyes beseeching, she whispered, "Kiss me. Please, Matt."

There was no triumph in his smile, only pleasure, and there was no hesitation in his response. His mouth slanted across her parted lips; his tongue, wet and searing, explored her greedily. And just as greedily she returned the pleasure. Her hands drifted lower, massaging the small indentation at the base of his spine, as their mouths, slippery with passion, clung, then parted breathlessly before starting the sweet duel all over again.

Soon his kiss alone was not enough to assuage her growing need. She needed—wanted—more of him in every way. There was no thought of caution or resistance now; all that had long since been swept away by the sheer intensity of her arousal. She dripped moist kisses across his cheek, his neck, the curve of his shoulder, tasting chlorine from the water and the faintly salty essence that was his.

He breathed softly in her ear, "Oh, Katie," then filled it with his tongue, rushing her senses with a new spasm of shivers.

Her breath came in short, shallow exhalations as she rolled her head back, relishing the slow trail his mouth was blazing down her throat to the tip of one breast. He circled it with his tongue and tugged gently, the sensation through the wet, clinging fabric intensely erotic. Then, seemingly impatient with even such a thin barrier, he dragged her shirt up and repeated the process on her bare skin.

For long, glorious moments she soared on the waves of sensation roused by his tender tugging and stroking, lost in the sweet world of sensual turbulence he'd set spinning.

Gently, his knee parted her thighs and slipped in between, riding up high against her. Kate gasped at the first thrilling contact, then began moving in an unthinking rhythm against the mild pressure. She nuzzled closer to his water-slicked body, balancing with hands on his shoulders to support her unsteady legs. Her mind cloudy with desire, she rubbed her cheek against his chest and breathed his name softly into its curling mat of bronze hairs.

With a soft moan he returned to her lips, concentrating his attention there while his fingers slipped to the zipper of her shorts. Patiently he worked the wet, stubborn metal until it slid open, admitting first a cool rush of water, and then his warm, searching fingers. He plied her with tenderly skillful motions, kindling a low, responsive cry from deep within her. It pleased Kate to feel him tremble at the sound.

Then his touch slipped away, and even as she whimpered in bewildered protest, he was lifting her up, holding her tightly against his chest. With her face pressed close to his neck she could feel him drawing in great, ragged gulps. Rather than aiming at her arousal, he now seemed to be gearing all his efforts toward bringing his own ravaging hunger under control . . . and having quite a time of it.

Confused, trembling somewhere between desire and frustration, Kate pulled away from him, a move he cooperated with only to a degree. He angled back and stared down into her face with its trembling lips and eyes opened wide in confusion, and the start of a sensual smile turned to a look of concern.

"Oh no, please, don't look at me like that. You don't understand." He heaved a sigh of pure self-disgust. "Lord, how could I expect you to understand? Katie, listen to me. Right now I want to take these wet clothes off you, and I want to kiss and pleasure every inch of you, but most of all . . ." He paused to draw a shaky breath. "You're probably going to think I'm crazy, but most of all, I want to take you home. I want the first time to be long and slow, with the stars shining through the skylight above my bed."

Dazed, her body still protesting the cessation of his magical ministrations, Kate only half heard what he said. Home? The word was an intrusion into the dreamy, time-suspended world where she was floating. His use of it seemed blatantly inappropriate. Home. To Matt, home wouldn't be the kind of old-fashioned sanctuary she'd grown up in, but a place to dash in and change clothes between constant business appointments, a place to grab a few hours' sleep and a quickie with the little woman whenever the urge for either became great enough. She'd had that kind of "home" with

Jeff. Did she really want it again?

No. Her hands left his shoulders and pressed a little frantically against his chest. "No."

At first his smile was warmly teasing, as if she were only resisting this momentary postponement and not the whole idea, him, everything. Kate watched as understanding slowly filtered into his overbright eyes, and with it an awesome desperation.

At that moment she felt acutely vulnerable, fearful of what he might do next. Isolated as they were, she would be powerless if he resorted to force. And, she realized dismally, she'd be almost as powerless if he chose to employ more intimate, already proven methods of firing her blood until her need was as urgent as it had been moments before.

He did neither. Looking slightly dazed himself, he asked wearily, "Why?"

Why. A slow welling of tears made his image waver before her. The reasons why were too convoluted, too jumbled in her own head to go into now. How could she explain that he was too much like Jeff, too reminiscent of her unhappy past, when at the moment he seemed anything but?

"It's just too soon," she said quietly, despising the weak reply for the cliché it was.

She felt even worse when, with a bitter laugh, he dropped his hands from her.

"Too soon? It sure as hell didn't feel like it was too soon. And these juices pumping inside my body"—he lightly jabbed her sternum with his index finger—"and inside yours, say it's not too soon."

She swallowed the tears in her throat, pressed the back of her wrists to her eyelids to stem a fresh resurgence there, and let the silence between them grow. He was right. But she was right, too. Maybe it wasn't too soon between them, but it was too risky . . . for her, anyway.

He pulled her hands away from her eyes and with one finger blotted the tears from her cheeks. "Okay."

Kate stared up at him, her eyes wide with disbelief. "Okay? Just like that?"

Like an old friend, the teasing, mustache-curling grin spread across his face. Before she knew what he was up to, he pulled her hard against him, rubbing his still-aroused body slowly against hers.

"No, if you must know, not just like that. But if you feel inclined to say it's too soon, it must be too soon." He let an insulating barrier of water seep between them once more and lifted her chin with his cupped palm. "Smile. Everything is going to be all right. I'm going to make it all right. And somehow I'm going to find a way to make you believe that."

Kate stared into his eyes, wishing she could tell for sure how deep, or how abiding, the promises she saw there were.

Sliding a strong arm around her shoulders, he kissed the top of her head. "Come on, let's go home."

Kate snuggled against his side, amazed at how much more comfortably the word *home* fit this time.

6

CROSSING TO THE counter at the front of the shop, Kate took a swig from a can of diet cola and crossed off one more entry on her list of things to do. As the column of neat pencil lines grew, so did her confidence that Sleepy Hollow would really be ready to open in eight days. Her thoughtful perusal of the remaining items on the list was interrupted by the tinkling of the tiny bell over the shop door. She'd been half expecting Matt to pop in all morning and was half disappointed when, instead, it turned out to be a teenage boy with straggly brown hair, torn jeans, and a ratty old sweatshirt.

"Hi ya," he mumbled, dragging his boot heels across the floor to where she stood at the end of the counter.

Kate smiled. "Good morning. Can I help you with something?"

"Yeah." He dug in the pocket of his jeans for a rumpled scrap of paper. "I'm here for the job. I saw your notice on the bulletin board in the post office."

Kate recognized the mauled paper he was holding up as the notice she'd so painstakingly printed, seeking a part-time clerk. "I guess you did more than just see it."

The calculated ice in her tone was wasted on the young man.

"Yeah. I couldn't see any sense in leaving it up there. I mean now that you've got me and all."

Got him? God help me, thought Kate, biting her lip to keep from blurting it out loud. "I'm sorry, but I don't think you're the right person for this particular job."

He tossed the paper on the counter in front of her. "It says here 'clerk.' Anyone can be a clerk."

"Perhaps, but I'm looking for someone with an interest in sewing or quilting. Do you know anything at all about quilts?"

The look he gave the quilts lying neatly folded behind her was distinctly unimpressed and uninterested. "What's to know? Somebody comes in, they buy one, I wrap it up and take their dough." His shoulders jerked up nonchalantly. "Piece of cake."

Kate was torn between the urge to laugh in his face and the desire to look skyward and demand "Why me?"

"I'm afraid there's quite a bit more to it than that." Her tone was now plainly dismissive. "I'm sure there are a lot of other summer positions on the island you'd be much better suited for."

Please just don't ask me to name one, she prayed. He didn't. Instead, he took a step closer, and Kate's attitude of amused indulgence faded in the face of a stare that was purely menacing.

"Yeah? And what if I said I thought I was suited for this job?"

"Then I'd say you'd better back away from the lady and do some rethinking, unless you want to buy a half dozen tickets to ferry all the pieces of you back to the mainland."

The familiar deep voice that had teased and taunted her and made her stomach flutter with desire when it lowered to a sensual purr now poured over Kate like a blanket of security.

The kid whirled to face the tall, solid man still holding the door open with one hand. "Who're you?"

Kate held her breath, noting the almost imperceptible clenching of Matt's jaw at the belligerent demand.

"I'm the man who owns the floor you're standing on. I'm also the man who's going to toss you out of here bodily if you don't leave under your own power. Now."

The corners of his mouth lifted, and Kate was surprised

to discover she already knew him well enough to identify what that half smiled masked: impatience, anger, and most of all awesome determination. For about ten seconds the young man vacillated, probably calculating his chances against Matt's threats. Then, displaying a degree of intelligence Kate wouldn't have credited him with, he swaggered out, mumbling, "Who'd want to work for such a . . ."

They were spared hearing his opinion of her by the door Matt slammed hard on his heels. He leaned against it and smiled reassuringly at her.

"Are you okay?"

"Yes. Thank you." The words rushed from Kate on a long sigh of relief.

"Thank you? That's it?" He crossed the shop with a couple of long strides, once more wearing the teasing expression she knew so well. "No eager signs of gratitude? No tearful embraces?" He shook his head disapprovingly. "I don't think this is the way Scarlett reacted when Rhett Butler saved her from being barbecued in Atlanta."

"You didn't rescue me from a city of burning buildings," she reminded him. "Just one rather obnoxious adolescent."

"A very dangerous species, the adolescent male—especially when rejected. Under the circumstances I think the least you can do is throw yourself in my arms and deliver a proper thank you."

Kate pursed her lips and made a great show of contemplating his suggestion. Throwing herself into his arms was an enticing idea—if a somewhat risky one—and not purely for reasons of gratitude. She finally settled for a safe, middle-of-the-road course and, taking him by surprise, threw her arms around his neck and planted a light peck on his lips. She broke away before he had a chance to react.

"Not bad," he drawled as she peered up at him, her eyes laughing, challenging. "Not what I'll expect if I ever have occasion to rescue you from a burning building, mind you, but all in all, not bad."

"Don't hold your breath; I'm very careful about playing with fire."

He pinned her with his gaze briefly, intently, before letting it wander aimlessly about the shop. "Are you? I would have said otherwise."

The reference to the night before was downright obvious,

making her flinch, toy nervously with the marking pencils lying on the counter waiting to be priced, and search her brain wildly for something—anything—to say to change the subject.

"Anyway, I'm glad you happened by when you did." She suddenly felt compelled to add, "Although I could have handled it by myself."

He grinned. "No doubt."

She lifted her chin. "I could have."

The indulgent grin grew even wider; he reached up and stroked the dark mustache with his thumb as if trying to bring the smile under control. "I'm not arguing with you."

Again he stood there, smiling at her, letting the silence between them roll on, and again she felt compelled to fill it.

"Did you? Just happen by, I mean, or did you stop by for a reason?" She held her breath, waiting for his answer, not quite sure which way she would prefer it.

"I suppose I should cover myself by making up some sensible reason for coming, but the truth is I just wanted to see you."

Kate felt her heart melting at the slightly sheepish, totally unexpected way he was looking at her.

His tone lowered, becoming almost confessional. "I wanted to wake you before I left for work this morning, but I talked myself out of it."

"You didn't leave me any message on the mirror." Hearing her own slightly husky tone, Kate wondered if she was simply commenting or complaining.

His smile was no more than a lopsided tilting of his mouth, slow, heart-wrenching. "All of a sudden the things I want to say to you aren't so easily handled with an aerosol can."

Touched by the admission, overwhelmed by the warmth in his clear, compelling blue eyes, her gaze slipped to his mouth, his broad chest, and then the patch of wooden floor between them.

"They're not so easily said in the middle of a quilt shop at high noon," he continued, "but I was going crazy out at the site, thinking of you, remembering last night, and wondering how you'd feel about it this morning."

She lifted her eyes to him, feeling a tingling sweetness she shouldn't be feeling. "I was hoping you'd stop by."

He let loose a deep chuckle that sounded like equal parts of delight and relief. "You just made my day. All the members of my crew thank you for putting a smile back on my face." Catching her hand in his, he led her to the back of the shop. "Speaking of crew, I've got to get back. But first, how's my workmanship holding up? Any complaints?"

"Just one tiny one. One of the nails in that corner bracket is coming loose. I'm afraid if I pull on that quilt it will come right out."

"Some of the mortar must have chipped away. That's easily remedied with a little filling compound. I think I've got some in the truck."

A minute later he was back, setting up the step ladder he'd left in the shop for her use. He was halfway up when Kate noticed the metal braces at the sides of the ladder hadn't been snapped fully open.

"Matt, I think you should check the ladder. You haven't got it up right."

He looked down at her with a smirk. "Kate, I work with ladders all day. It's fine."

She eyed the ladder dubiously. It seemed to sway a bit as he reached for the troublesome nail. "Really, Matt, I wish you'd just come down and take a look."

His reply was distorted by the nail he held in his teeth. "Don't worry. This will only take another—"

The rest of his pronouncement became a savage oath as the ladder snapped shut, sending Matt tumbling to the ground, a vivid red and yellow quilt billowing around him like a parachute. It was immediately obvious he'd suffered no real damage, and Kate's question was tinged with laughter.

"Are you okay?"

He glared up at her. "No, I'm not okay. I'm totally humiliated."

She surveyed his sprawled form smugly. "It's not exactly the sort of thing I picture happening to Rhett Butler."

She had to let out the bubble of laughter before she choked on it. There seemed to be a responding chuckle trying to force its way through Matt's grimace, despite his injured tone.

"Well, Scarlett, if you can pull yourself together for a minute, maybe you could give me a hand getting up from here." He paused, then explained in disgust, "I seem to be caught on something."

With a smile as broad as a barn door, she slowly walked toward him, slowly lifted the quilt and folded it neatly, then leaned closer to determine the source of his problem.

"You're stuck, all right," she announced after an unnecessarily long inspection.

"I know that. Just get me unstuck."

His hand came around and began tugging impatiently at the spot where his belt had hooked onto the ladder's broken metal brace.

"You're not helping," she admonished.

"Neither are you."

"Well, if you'd get your big fingers out of the way—"

"Right now I'd like to wrap my big fingers around your little neck."

She pretended to straighten up. "If you're going to be peevish . . ."

"I'm not," he assured her quickly. "See, I'm even smiling."

She glanced approvingly at the stiff, exaggerated curl of his lips. "That's much better."

With one deft movement she freed his belt, and he sprang to his feet, whirling to face her with eyes flashing.

"Think you're pretty cute, don't you?"

Kate saw the playfulness lurking beneath his ferocious expression and refused to retreat as he took one, then another slow, menacing step closer.

Feigning dismay, she batted her eyelashes up at him and purred. "What? No tearful thanks? No flowery expressions of gratitude? I'm devastated by your lack of sensitivity."

"So, now it's sensitivity you want from me? What happened to businesslike and professional?" Before she could do more than blink, he changed tacks completely. "But you know, you're absolutely right. I should be on my knees to you. There's no telling what wretched fate I might have met if you hadn't acted to save my life." As Kate eyed him suspiciously, he stepped closer, obviously warming to his soliloquy. "I might have starved to death here, trapped, alone. Or even worse, been eaten by a pack of wandering mice."

"There are no mice in here," she pointed out dryly.

"That's why I said wandering," he countered. "You never know when they might come..."

"Wandering in," she finished with a groan.

He nodded. "Precisely. But you spared me all that, with no thought to your own life or limb."

Playing along, Kate gave a grand shrug. "It was nothing."

"No, no. I won't let you make light of it. You saved my life, and now, from this moment on, forever after"—his eyes came alight in a way that sent wary shivers rushing through her—"I'm yours."

Aiming for a lightness she no longer felt, she smiled up and down the tantalizing length of him. "That's very generous of you, but I'm afraid I can't accept."

"You have to. It's a very old, authentic Chinese proverb."

"Very old," she echoed, most of her mind drifting on the currents of sensuality he was emitting.

"Just think," he continued with rapture so phony it started her laughing all over again, "bound for all eternity, two souls permanently linked because of one fleeting act of bravery."

She pondered that for a moment. "Do you think I could just have a monetary reward instead?"

His features contracted into a bogus frown. "Woman, you have no soul."

"No... but I do have tons of work to do today." She retrieved his can of filling compound and slapped it into his hand. "Good-bye, Matt."

He tossed the can into the air and caught it, making no move for the door. "You could persuade me to leave..."

"I thought I just did."

"By agreeing to let me take you out to dinner after work as a token of my gratitude."

"Another noble offer, but I never eat dinner after midnight. It spoils my breakfast."

"I've got things pretty well under control at work. I think I could manage to knock off earlier tonight. Say, six o'clock?"

Kate hesitated, wanting more than anything to have dinner with him, and knowing with an innate certainty what such a capitulation, coming after last night, would signify.

"Come on, Kate. You owe it to yourself after slaving over a hot oven every night this week." His smile held knowing amusement. "I saw the TV-dinner boxes in the trash." Much more quietly he added, "Please don't play games with me, Kate."

His tone was gently pleading, and all her well-honed reservations collapsed like a pup tent in a hurricane. "I'll have dinner with you."

As if afraid her surrender might be fleeting, he broke for the door. "Great. I'll be home in time to grab a quick shower and change clothes." He paused to glance sheepishly at the dowel hanging loose above her head and at the broken ladder. "I'll...uh, send a carpenter over to take care of all that."

The carpenter he sent, a squat redhead named Jack Sutton, was there when the flowers arrived three hours later. Not that he even would have noticed the arrival of the long, glossy white box if it had been delivered by anyone other than Roger, the handyman down at the ferry landing and self-appointed head of the island gossip mill.

"Rushed these right up to you the second the ferry docked," he announced smugly, placing the box on the counter in front of Kate. "You know what's inside?"

"I will in a minute," she replied, feeling a rush of excitement as she reached for the small card tucked under the ribbon and wishing Roger would shove off.

"Long-stemmed roses," he informed her. "Red roses. American beauties."

Ignoring him, she read the card, smiling at the simple inscription, "To my heroine, Love, Matt." Inside, the roses lay cushioned on green tissue, their petals like rich crimson velvet.

"Whew!" Roger's reaction was an echo of her own. "There must be two dozen of them in there. You know what those babies cost to have ferried over here? Plenty. Last time I knew of anyone to do it was Doc Hendricks—the day after he got loaded at the Harvest supper and told everyone his wife's five years older than him. Even then, he only sent one dozen. What did that Kincade fellow do to cost him this?"

Climbing down from the newly repaired ladder, Jack Sutton ambled over to them, attracted by the mention of his boss's name as he hadn't been by the flowers alone. "Did you say Kincade? Matt Kincade?"

Roger nodded. "That's the one. And you can bet these cost him a pretty penny." He poked the other man in the ribs conspiratorially. "Paying the piper, if you know what I mean."

The sight of the two of them chuckling, perfectly content to stand there discussing her personal life at length, sent Kate scurrying for her purse. Grabbing the first money she spotted—a five-dollar bill—she thrust it at Roger.

"Thanks, Roger. I'll put them in water right away."

Reluctantly, he let himself be hustled out the door, and, just as reluctantly, the carpenter returned to work. Arranging the roses in a plastic pail, Kate lingered over each bud, savoring their scent, caressing the downy soft petals with gentle fingertips.

The delight she took in the labor was a surprise. Roses had been a frequent gift from Jeff during their marriage, but not even in the early days, when she still believed in their love, had she experienced this tangle of leaping emotions brought on by Matt's flowers.

Slowly, as the roses in the pail grew into a gently leaning bouquet, it dawned on her that, for all their similarities, Matt was as different from Jeff as Block Island was from Santa Monica. And the differences ran far deeper than the unprecedented sensual impact Matt had on her. Like a fresh, clear morning, Matt seemed to hold the promise of all sorts of wondrous things, like laughter shared, and the gift of self freely given. The sort of things whose absence rendered her marriage to Jeff nothing more than a pretty shell; the sort of things that stoked some long-neglected, suddenly restless yearning deep within her.

She abruptly stabbed the last rose into place and wiped her damp palms on her jeans. She must be crazy. Jeff was no prize, but they had been married, and here she was comparing him to a man she hardly knew. But, even as she told herself otherwise, some inner voice declared that she already knew Matt, and knew him in an intrinsic, elemental way that transcended the need to know where he went to high school or what kind of ice cream he liked best. All her laughing at his claims of a spiritual link between them couldn't alter the fact that it was beginning to feel exactly that way, or that when he smiled at her with that breath-stealing, sensuous curve of his mouth, its slow-lifting corners seemed to be tied right to the strings of her heart.

Later, dancing on the moonlit deck behind the Island Inn, Kate stared up into the deep violet eyes above that smile. Matt pursed his lips and blew gently at the strands of gold that had escaped her loose topknot.

"You look beautiful with roses in your hair."

Her hand lifted to the single bloom she'd tucked behind her ear at the last moment. "It was an impulse."

"Then you should learn to act on impulse more often."

His implication was not lost on her. She smiled up at him. "And you should learn to restrain yours. Roger, the guy who delivered the roses, said such gallant gestures will lighten your wallet considerably. He also wondered what indiscretion you'd committed to require sending them in the first place." Her smile deepened at the mild amusement that filled his eyes. "And all this in front of a very interested Jack Sutton."

Matt sighed with mock dismay. "Word of my infatuation will be all over the site by morning."

"Well, if it is, you can't hold poor Jack solely responsible. You may not know it, but around these less-than-liberated parts, the way you're holding me is tantamount to making an annoucement."

If anything, he tightened his arms around her, gliding his fingers over the silklike gauze of her dress, and bent his head to whisper, "Are we talking about a proper or improper announcement?"

Kate's shoulders lifted with laughter. "I think that's determined by how quickly the announcement is followed by tangible evidence of your affection . . . something simple and tasteful, like a rock the size of Mohegan Bluffs. If said evidence is not forthcoming, we will be said to have engaged in behavior that will, as my grandmother used to say, make me better known than soap."

He chuckled out loud at that, drawing curious smiles from several nearby couples. "What exactly does it mean to be better known than soap?"

Kate shrugged, her smile mysterious. "Beats me, but as kids it was enough to make Meg and me cut out whatever mischief we were up to immediately."

He nuzzled the gilted softness of her hair. "There's only one thing that could make me stop what I'm doing at this moment." Permitting the smallest of spaces between them, he tilted his head until his shining, eager gaze met hers. "Are you ready to come home with me now, Kate?"

7

SHE HAD, OF COURSE, known this moment would come.

The inevitability of it had haunted her while she debated which dress to wear; it had lurked about the fringes of her consciousness during the short drive from the lighthouse to the inn. Even during dinner, while they laughed at each other's clumsy efforts at cracking lobster tails, it had been there, with the flickering intensity of the hurricane-globed candles that wreathed the small dance floor.

She had not, however, expected her moment of decision to arrive so softly. Under Matt's patient, expectant gaze, it seemed an extraordinarily fragile thing, as delicate as the soapy bubbles children send billowing skyward on summer days. The soft strains of the music had faded away, and still he held her, his eyes hopeful yet devoid of any pressure.

Her fingers brushed down from his shoulders to rest against his chest. With his breath coming in short, warm gusts against her cheek, she gave him a small smile and the only answer possible.

"Yes, Matt. I'm ready to go."

The moments that followed might have been strained, unbearly awkward, but Matt made it all so easy, so natural. Later, Kate could hardly remember walking to the car, or driving back to the lighthouse, or even if they talked on the way. She did remember the heavy sensation of floating and melting at the same time, melting with a slow burn that Matt fed steadily with warm, lingering touches and short, stolen kisses.

She only dimly registered passing through the kitchen for the chilled wine he offered her when they reached his room at the top of the tower.

"No more for me." Her voice was breathy, slightly husky. "I'm already dizzy. My heart is racing."

Matt placed the unopened bottle on a shelf beside him and just stared at her, a thoroughly captivated expression on his face at what she had just so openly admitted to him. He was standing near the bed, bathed in the soft silver glow that streamed through the skylight. Night had turned the large windows encircling the room into inky mirrors that reflected them hazily from every angle.

Slowly he walked toward her, and the breath caught in her throat from the force of the longing that was a low, steady swelling deep inside her. This was the truly inevitable moment. Inevitable and irresistible. To resist would be as futile as trying to swim against the riptides that surged along the island's eastern shore. Futile gestures were the last thing on Kate's mind as Matt held his hand out to her with a look that was an intoxicating blend of adoration and desire.

"Let me feel your racing heart."

Moving at a snail's pace, feeding her anticipation and his, she carried his hand to where her heartbeat thundered. With gentle pressure his palm teased the slope of her breast. They both gave a low gasp of pleasure at the first thrilling touch, then chuckled together softly.

"Mmm. Definitely racing," he whispered. "It must have something to do with the altitude; mine's racing, too." The circular massage of his palm gave way to the lightly tantalizing, much more precise movements of his steady fingers. "And all of a sudden I'm finding it hard to catch my breath."

He had leaned steadily closer until the last word was breathed between her slightly parted lips, a heartbeat before his mouth closed over them. It was a dawdling kiss, more tinder for the fires of their mounting anticipation. He rocked his mouth against hers, used his full bottom lip to nudge hers farther apart; then, with the tip of his tongue he traced the moist flesh inside.

Hunger surged through her. She arched against him, unable to get enough of the delight of his lips, the sweet stroking of his fingers. The eagerness of her response unleashed a similar urgency in Matt. This time his mouth claimed hers hotly, demandingly—a demand Kate met willingly. She melted against him as his hands swept over her, lavishing caresses on her tautened breasts, her belly, her trembling thighs. One hand burned its way up to cradle her head, holding her still for the kiss that was no longer a gentle, courting gesture but a fiery branding of slow, erotic tongue thrusts.

He robbed her of her breath and at the same time lost his own. When he finally broke away to string a chain of kisses over her hair, they were both gasping.

His mustache tickled her ear as he spoke. "Oh, Kate, you smell good . . . you feel good . . . too good. Please help me go slowly."

Kate molded her supple curves closer to his hardness and smoothed her hands up and down his back, loving the strength she felt in him and amazed by her own lack of self-consciousness. With Jeff, it had always been there, along with the subtle need to perform in order to capture his interest and attention. She felt none of that now. There was no doubt she had Matt's full, undivided attention, and all she felt was a need to give, to return the pleasure she was drowning in.

Stretching to tiptoes, she kissed the pulse spot at the side of his throat, then let her tongue peek out to moisten his skin. "Am I helping?" she murmured, smiling up at him.

His eyes drifted shut, then opened, passion darkened. "Not even a little bit."

She licked her lips thoughtfully before reaching to peel off his jacket, then tug loose the silk tie. As her fingers gracefully liberated each shirt button in turn, feather-brushing his hard chest in the process, she whispered, "How about this?"

His answer came on a deep groan. "I don't think so."

She had the shirt off now. Placing her palms flat on his

chest, she stroked with deep, sensual swirls and turns. She loved the feel of him, the hair-roughened texture of his skin, the supple layers of muscle over bone. She circled the flat nipples hidden beneath the curling bronze hairs, then trailed her fingers lower to dip provocatively just inside the waistband of his slacks. She felt his stomach muscles convulse under her gentle touch.

She had to try very hard to appear innocent. "I really don't know what else I can do to help."

Slowly, with delicious menace, the smile she loved spread across his face, lifting the dark mustache in the most tantalizing way. "Don't you now? Then I suppose I'll just have to show you."

A sweet shiver of anticipation coursed through her, and then Matt was kissing her with heart-bursting insistency. So lost was she in his magic that she didn't realize he'd undone the flimsy ties over her shoulders until the top of her dress slipped to her waist. He crushed her to him, the sensation of his rough chest against her soft breasts electrifying. Then, weaning his mouth from hers, he leaned back, worshiping with his eyes the treasure he'd unveiled.

The heat of his gaze made her nipples harden and all the rest of her turn pliant. She was melting in the heat of his flame, turning all moist and drizzly. He angled closer, trailing his hands along the sides of her ribs to cup her breasts, testing their weight, their fit in his palms, with an expression of awe.

Kate moaned softly as his head lowered. His breath was a soft, warm mist on her skin. Then his lips closed over her lightly, nibbling, teasing, flicking with a soothing tongue, until first one, then the other nipple swelled with longing. He slipped to one knee, looking up to meet her eyes with a gaze that was strong and sensuous. With leisurely, mesmerizing movements, he slid her dress lower, over her hips, her legs. Instinctively, she braced one hand on his shoulder as he helped her step out of it, leaving her clad only in a lacy half-slip, panties of apricot lace, and her sandals.

"Now your shoes, love," he directed softly.

Obediently, she lifted one foot after the other as he slipped off the sandals and tossed them behind him. Her heart doubled its pace as, with an unhurried touch, he stroked her calves, her suddenly shaky knees, and her thighs, both inside and out. She swayed helplessly, and his hands were there to catch her hips and steady her. He was an anchor, solid flesh and sinew in a world of dizzying sensation.

"Please, Matt." It was part entreaty, part silken demand.

"Shhh. You're supposed to be helping me take it slow . . . Remember? We have all night, and I plan to make full use of it. By morning you're going to be convinced of how right this is between us."

Kate peered at him from under her lashes, hips rolling with the gentle kneading motion of his hands. "I think I'm already convinced."

He shook his head and laughed softly. "But not as convinced as you will be. I'm going to love you until I wipe everything else from your mind. They say you can't stop time, but tonight I'm going to stop the world and spend infinity with you."

His arms stretched upward until his hands once again captured her breasts, his touch deft, gentle.

With a restless, arching motion, she rolled her head back. "Oh yes, Matt, yes."

"As much as you want, love, for as long as you want." His voice was a sensuous throb. "Then, when you're as hot as I am right now, when we're both on fire . . ." He slid up to whisper in her ear a most enticing proposition.

She giggled, clinging to the solid wall of his shoulders. "Why, Rhett, you rascal. I don't think nice people do that kind of thing."

Beneath the soft mustache, his mouth twisted in a lazy, faintly challenging grin. "So what do you want, lady? You wanna be nice, or you wanna have some fun?"

They laughed, great happy peals that ended abruptly when she reached up to cup his face with her hands.

"I want you."

It was an admission, an invitation, an out-and-out acknowledgment that what they were doing was fine and good.

He shook her gently, a soft smile in his voice. "Haven't you noticed? You have me . . . have had me since the moment you came barreling into my life."

She stared up at him, her smile growing wide and sassy, the undulating of her hips blatantly provocative. "Mmmm, but now I really want you."

Grinning like a kid on Christmas morning, Matt scooped

her up and carried her to his bed. She nibbled on his ear as he strode across the room, and she clung to his neck as he lowered her to the center of the woven blue spread, emitting a low, moaning complaint when he broke away.

"Patience is a virtue," he laughingly admonished, quickly shucking his pants and the rest of his clothes before covering her own eager body with his magnificently naked one. "Unfortunately, I've used all mine up."

He started at the ultrasensitive spot at the base of her throat and worked his way downward, leaving a legacy of moist kisses that scorched her skin. By the time he reached the elastic waistband of her slip and panties and started easing them down, she was trembling with desire, aching with the need to take what he offered and give it back to him.

Her thoughts were hazy, her movements born of instinct. She ran her hands over him, stroking and petting, marveling at the fine definition of his muscles, the way they rippled and flexed as he continued his abandoned exploration of her body. Lost in a glorious daze, she opened her eyes to the broad expanse of sky visible through the skylight above. Viewed through the misty fringe of her lashes, the stars above seemed engaged in a swirling dance, like snowflakes in a blizzard, each one as special and unique as the myriad sensations Matt's touch set spinning inside her.

When his wandering fingers and passion-slick lips had moved near and around and above the center of her desire until she thought she couldn't stand another second of such sweet agony, he rolled to his side full length beside her. He propped himself up on one elbow and with his other hand, gently and without a trace of hesitation, parted her legs.

She thrust up in welcome, responding with a natural, age-old rhythm as the heel of his hand pressed against her moist warmth. His name fell from her lips in a whispered chant as his fingers teased her with knowing movements, always couched in gentleness, until she was hovering on the edge of enchantment. As if sensing the fervor of her arousal, Matt slowed the tempo of his caress, then raised his hands to her shoulders and lightly rolled to cover her once more.

Breathing deeply with desire and expectation, Kate stared

up into his darkened blue eyes, the longing that simmered in them arousing her even more. Slowly, his knees found their place between hers. With a small gasp Kate tightened her arms around him and watched his eyes half close as he entered her with a slow, easy thrust.

He moved slowly, inviting her to learn the rhythm of his passion and join in, and she did. She felt a gradual, steady tightening of everything inside her, and the real world seemed to recede, becoming as distant and out of reach as the stars suspended above.

Never at any moment in her life had Kate felt this incredible sense of harmony. The borders delineating her body from Matt's, her movements and pleasure from his, blurred into nonexistence. The fingers resting lightly on his shoulders began to clench as their tempo increased and with it the straining within. It was the same thrilling, deliciously tense feeling she got in the pit of her stomach on the Ferris wheel—only magnified a million times.

Eagerly she accepted the white-hot thrusts of his tongue. The kiss was frenzied, uncoordinated, at variance with the highly choreographed rocking of their hips. His lips journeyed to her ear, whispering words of love and desire, as she climbed higher and higher, faster and faster. Then she was plummeting over the top, cascading back to earth with a long, low moan of pleasure that found a masculine echo in Matt's groan of fulfillment.

For a time they clung together, joined by the veil of dampness coating their bodies and a shared, saturating contentment. Eyes closed, Kate smiled and wiggled her toes, basking in this newly discovered feeling that transcended happiness, this peaceful blend of joy and satisfaction. She felt as though she'd moved from stormy seas into a sweet, safe harbor.

Matt rolled to his side, still hugging her close, and covered her giddy toes with his foot. "Restless?"

She opened her eyes and smiled into his. "Nope. Just happy."

He chuckled, an eminently satisfied and, to Kate, satisfying, sound. "We were good, weren't we?"

"Good? We were great. I saw stars."

He broke into a triumphant grin. Then he followed her

pointed gaze to the sparkling galaxy visible above and twisted her for a playful slap on the fanny. "You're heartless. Here I was thinking my loving inspired your celestial visions."

She looked at him out of the corner of her eye. "I guess we'll just have to try harder."

"Okay." He grasped her wrists and rolled to his back, pulling her along until she fell across his chest, straddling him. "Only this time, I want to see stars."

Her eyes widened incredulously. "This time? You can't mean . . ."

Her question trailed off as he positioned her carefully and proceeded to rub against her most convincingly. "You want to bet?"

Kate opened her eyes in a room ablaze with apricot sunshine. Lying by her side, Matt seemed blissfully immune to the rousing powers of the brilliant morning sun. She chuckled softly, remembering the wild, abandoned night that had tuckered him so.

The urge to laugh quickly dissipated into a heavy sigh as an army of morning-after demons made their appearance. She tugged the sheet higher and tried to sort out what was happening inside. She should definitely be feeling something—confusion, guilt, anger at Matt for his dogged pursuit and at herself for allowing it to come to this. But, shamefully, she felt none of those things, only a lingering trace of excitement, and a languorous contentment that made her stretch kittenishly.

Memories of the heavenly sensations evoked by his warm, searching lips and callused fingertips brought a smile to her, and, rolling to her side, she observed him over the plump edge of her pillow, a little amazed at the discovery that she wanted him all over again. For so long sexual desire had been a nonentity in her life. That lack of desire had seemed an understandable and, Kate had hoped, temporary outgrowth of the months of cold war with Jeff.

Now she feasted her eyes on Matt, his skin a copper sheen against the white sheet. Her sexual apathy had proved temporary, all right. Only why did Matt have to be the man to end it? She'd had it all figured out, broken down to lowest common denominators: a healthy life-plan for what she did and didn't need for future happiness. And number one on her "not needed" list was this year's version of the man she'd already had. She couldn't even plead ignorance. She'd known from the start that Matt had both feet firmly planted on the pathway to wealth and power. And, save for the night before, his long hours at the site had proved it over and over again. That path seemed to Kate a treadmill, one she'd made a painful leap off and had no intention of climbing back onto.

She pondered how, after such a brilliantly intuitive analysis of the situation, she'd managed to wind up in the bed of a man who was all wrong for her. The answer was achingly simple, coming to her as spontaneously as the urge to stroke his whisker-darkened cheek. She had wanted it to happen, had wanted him, as fiercely and desperately as Matt's fiery possession had shown he wanted her.

He shifted beside her, and Kate felt a rush of affection as she watched him sleepily scratching his hairy chest with the back of one big hand. The desire to reach out and touch him, to brush the soft chestnut lock from his forehead, became a physical ache, alarming in its intensity. Last night in the glorious haze of passion, it had been easy not to think beyond the moment. Unfortunately, what had been so pure and simple just hours ago now seemed involved and complicated, an incredibly tangled web of emotions.

Slipping from the bed, she pulled on the white shirt she'd taken such pleasure in stripping off him last night and left Matt still sleeping.

A short time later, dressed in blue cotton slacks and a yellow oxford shirt in deference to the breezy morning, she brought her coffee out onto the deck and tried to work on the Dresden Plate pillow top she was quilting. The execution of the neat, orderly stitches kept her fingers occupied but left her mind free to worry and fret and compose long lists of regrets that were rendered useless the instant Matt strolled onto the deck. She took one look at the eager smile on his roughly handsome face and knew that what she felt for him was nothing as simple and uncomplicated as lust.

"You left me." His tone was mildly accusing as he squatted in front of her, but his expression and the warm fingers that strayed just inside the open collar of her shirt were yearning, hungry, and all for her.

He leaned closer to kiss her, a nibbling, licking melding of tongues that filled more than her mouth. It filled dark, deep places in her soul that Kate hadn't even known were empty.

"You were sleeping," she explained with a shiver as his lips wandered to bid a moist good morning to the rest of her face. "I didn't want to wake you."

"Next time, wake me," he ordered gruffly, tickling the tip of her nose with his mustache.

Next time? Of course there would be a next time, and a time after that. She wasn't naive enough to think either of them could resume the "strictly business" facade after last night. How on earth was she going to handle this?

With a light touch, she decided quickly, calling all her instincts for survival to the fore. Even if inside she was a bundle of raw nerves, poised on the brink of falling head over heels, she'd do her darnedest to keep up an appearance of superficiality.

"Next time?" she asked, her smile teasingly sultry. "Kind of sure of yourself, aren't you?"

He levered back on his heels, catching her hands in his and squeezing tightly. "I'd much rather be sure of you."

"Never. A woman likes to retain an air of mystery."

He didn't smile at her Hungarian accent. "Do you want to play verbal hide and seek, or can we talk about it?"

"About what?" Her accelerated heartbeat was only partly due to the way his fingers were stroking her damp palms.

"About the reason you look like someone who's trying to smile bravely after receiving the worst news of her life. The phone hasn't rung, and I don't think you've been out yet this morning, so that means the bad news must be me."

Her protest was automatic, coming straight from her pounding heart. "No, not you."

The visible relaxation of his body revealed a vulnerability Kate hadn't suspected. "Thank God. I was frantic, thinking you woke up, took one look at the toad lying next to you, and bolted."

Kate smiled, on the verge of telling him how far off base he was, when he continued.

"That leaves us with comparatively simple problems to

solve, such as, I suspect, a tidal wave of uneasiness over what happened last night." He leaned forward, resting their entwined hands deep in her lap. His expression was earnest, reassuring. "There's no need to feel uneasy, Kate, or ashamed, or any of those other required morning-after emotions."

She smiled. "I'm not. Don't you recognize a liberated woman when you bed one?"

The concern in his eyes grabbed at her heart as he placed gentle fingers on her lips. "Be quiet. What I'm going to say is going to sound premature. It's going to sound that way, but it's not. I love you, Kate." He grinned exuberantly. "I'm as sure of that as I am that you're going to fight the whole idea tooth and nail. I love you, and I want to spend the rest of my life with you."

A wellspring of pure happiness erupted inside her at the declaration, followed immediately by an equally forceful thrust of anguish. His admission of love had not come lightly, of that she was certain. This was no obligatory effort to soothe the morning-after guilties of a bedmate; nor was it the impetuous ranting of a love-struck adolescent.

Matt was a man, a very desirable one. Beyond that, Kate still wasn't sure what she felt for him, but she was sure that if he ever suspected how far her feelings leaned in the direction of his own, he would become an even more irresistible force. She let her gaze stray to her sandals, the deck railing, a small patch of sky over his right shoulder. At last she looked into his patient blue eyes and offered him a shaky smile.

"The rest of your life could be a very long time."

"Not nearly long enough."

"I can't even cook."

He grinned, and in an unexpected, thoroughly audacious move, reached up to caress her breasts. "True. But you have compensatory talents."

Under his bold touch she felt desire, a hot, violent gush of it, and pushed his hands away. Her laugh sounded forced, brittle. "This is crazy. We've known each other less than two weeks."

His censured hands wandered down her legs to encircle her ankles. "It took me that long to be absolutely sure. I strongly suspected I was in love with you the day you came to see me at the site, but I didn't want to rush things."

"God forbid." She uttered the words with an attempt at a droll smile. His own rivaled the sun for brilliance and sent her skyrocketing.

"Marry me."

How to be slammed back to earth with two little words. "I'd love to," she said with false cheeriness, "but I have a dentist appointment. Maybe some other time."

"Don't."

He was on his feet, stalking across the deck to grip the railing, straight-armed. The muscles in his back flexed tensely, and Kate held her breath. She had a feeling the traces of irritation she'd seen up till now wouldn't hold a candle to his anger at this moment. But, when he turned back to face her, she wished anger was all she read on his face. Anything would be better than seeing it lined with pain and knowing she was responsible.

"Don't do that to me." Her stomach twisted into a knot at his hushed tone. "Don't use one of your damned clever comebacks to avoid me. If you're not sure, say you're not sure. If you're scared, say you're scared. But don't make a joke out of my love for you."

Hearing it put so bluntly, knowing it was all too true, she felt a wave of remorse, and at its crest, a fierce need to make things right between them.

He didn't look so tough now; he looked more like a little boy who'd just offered someone his most prized treasure and had it tossed back in his face. How could she have been so blind to the level of vulnerability beneath that hard-driving exterior? She'd been so busy scrambling to disguise her own tumultuous feelings, she hadn't bothered to consider his.

The spell of silence stretched traumatically while she searched for some way to erase the hurt look from his eyes. At the moment, the need to see his smile surpassed all others, propelling her across the deck to his side.

"I'm sorry. I really wasn't trying to make a joke of it." She started to raise unsteady hands to his shoulders, then stopped short. Last night she'd made love with the man, and now she felt too self-conscious to comfort him with her touch.

The quick twist of his lips was not even close to the smile Kate longed for. "You sure could have fooled me."

"Okay, maybe I did make a joke of it, but what did you expect? You caught me off guard."

"But never speechless," he added, his tone cynical.

"I'm sorry. I wasn't expecting a marriage proposal over morning coffee."

He took a hard breath, glaring at her. "No? Then tell me, what do you usually hear over coffee after a night like last night?"

8

SHE MET HIS snapping gaze head-on, her voice quiet and serious. "I don't know. I've never had a night like last night before in my whole life."

Matt's eyes closed briefly. His breath came out in a long, low whoosh, and the first hint of a smile appeared below the still-drooping mustache. "Hearing you admit that is almost worth this whole lousy argument." Long, strong fingers encircled her upper arms, squeezing carefully. "Why are we arguing anyway?"

"I don't know." Then, in confusion, she added, "I don't know what you want from me."

"Right now I want to know how you feel." His eyes narrowed in a premature rebuff. "The truth."

Ignoring her instinct to be wary of any man who could plumb the depths of her heart with nothing more than a longing look, Kate expelled the breath lodged in her throat and went ahead and told him the truth. "I'm not sure. And I'm scared." She paused. "And worried."

The concern that filtered into his eyes warmed her as the summer sun never could. "Don't be. I know it's natural for a woman to be concerned, especially when things happen so quickly. Last night was no one-night stand; I fully intend to marry you."

She gave a hollow laugh. If only her worries were that simple. "That's exactly what worries me. If you came down here this morning, slapped me on the backside, and said 'Thanks for a swell time, honey,' I would have been furious, but in the long run it would have made things easier for both of us."

The hands that had been gently kneading her shoulders fell still as he listened intently.

"This"—she waved her hand with a frown—"is only going to complicate things."

For a moment Matt looked utterly bewildered, and Kate wished she'd never started this bungling attempt to explain. Then he nodded, shades of sarcasm skulking beneath his knowing look.

"Of course. I should have known my fast-track West Coast lady would never be worried over anything as provincial as a marriage proposal." He hitched one foot on the lower rail and crossed his arms in front of him. "I don't suppose it would influence your feelings at all if I suggested we could make things work in spite of our vastly different lifestyles?"

Kate heaved an exasperated sigh. "The only difference in our lifestyles is that I've already been where you're headed . . . and I don't want to go back there again. I don't need anything I left behind to make me happy." She couldn't miss the disbelief that clouded his eyes. "Why can't you believe that?"

His smile was softly self-reproaching. "Probably because it's so damn important to me. Because I want so badly for it to be true, and the things I want badly never come easy for me."

Kate's eyes widened. She would have guessed that everything came easy for Matt, and to hear him quietly claim otherwise raised a host of questions. Before she could ask even one of them, he caught her in a quick hug that lifted her feet off the deck and swung her in circles as effortlessly as the morning breeze carried the misty spray from the sea. When she was breathless from laughing and helplessly, clingingly dizzy, he put her down.

"Let's forget all this. Bringing it up in the first place was probably an error in timing on my part. Consider the marriage offer temporarily withdrawn." His tone was light;

his grin crinkled the corners of his eyes. "In its place, I have a substitute, one I'm sure you'll find a whole lot more tempting. I have to meet with my lawyer this afternoon, and I want to stop home and pick up my mail while I'm there. Keep me company on the ferry, and I'll take you out to dinner afterward. You can get in some heavy shopping in those fancy Watch Hill boutiques." He shook his head at her eager smile. "I knew that would get through to you."

Happy to be basking in his smile once again, Kate overlooked the sly insinuation about shopping and accepted.

Wandering through the boutiques that lined the narrow, picturesque streets of the seaside town of Watch Hill, Kate wondered if she looked as confused as she felt. She should be walking on air, or at least feeling pleasantly flattered that a man as attractive and desirable as Matt claimed to be in love with her. Instead, she was stuck right in the middle, pulled one way by the past experience and another by the inner urging to throw caution to the wind and trust him. For now, she would continue to fight her instincts . . . and his. But she had to wonder how a gambler would lay the odds, when an increasingly large part of her was fighting on Matt's side.

He was waiting when she returned to his lawyer's office, leaning against the granite wall outside, his shirt a broad flash of white between his tanned face and the snug-fitting black denims. His clothes and his stance lent him decidedly buccaneer overtones that weren't lost on Kate.

He smiled when he opened the box of fudge that was her only purchase. "Thank you, but if this is a ploy to distract me from the sweetness I really crave, it's bound to be a dismal failure." He kissed her lips lightly. "Is this all you bought?" Disbelief was rife in his tone and his slightly arched brows.

"I'm having the rest delivered; I had to hire a small oceanliner to hold everything." She fluttered her lashes at him coquettishly. "And I charged all the purchases to you. I hope you don't mind."

The teasing glimmer in his eyes was shadowed. "Believe me, darlin', the spirit is willing, but my financial situation is suddenly a bit precarious."

It wasn't the sort of light response she expected. His

tone was subdued, devoid of the tantalizing lilt that usually threaded through its roughness. Kate looked him over more carefully and noticed the weariness beneath the weak smile, the uncharacteristic sag to his posture.

"How did your meeting go?" she asked, already knowing the answer just by looking at him.

"From bad to worse . . . and then some."

For a second she hesitated, not knowing what she should ask or how much or even if it was any of her business. Then a lifetime of polite restraint was shattered by the surge of protectiveness she felt toward this man. She looped her arm through his, smoothing the tense muscles of his forearm with her fingers.

"Tell me about it."

He brightened a bit, more out of gratitude than cheer, she suspected, and she was glad she'd decided to forget her manners.

"I'll tell you the whole depressing story over dinner. I'm afraid it will have to be someplace informal." He ran his eyes pointedly over his own casual attire, then hers, and Kate, warmed by the flicker of approval in his eyes, would have been more than willing to eat in the greasy spoon of his choice.

The small outdoor café they discovered just up the street was not at all greasy. The fringe on the overhead umbrella swayed in the mild breeze as they perused the menu's hundred and sixty-seven humorously named sandwich offerings. They both decided on something called Three Coins in a Mountain, and over thick, knotted rolls overflowing with turkey, ham, and cheese, Matt started talking.

"It's a nightmare. Short of an earthquake or a fire ravaging the island, it's the absolute worst thing that could have happened." He shook his head with a short, cynical laugh. "I take it back; it's the worst thing. At least my insurance would have covered earthquake damage."

"Are you going to tell me what happened, or are we playing twenty questions?"

He ran impatient fingers through his hair, leaving it endearingly tousled. "I'm sorry. One of the island town committeemen, Gus Rennack, has proposed an ordinance to limit the changes of occupancy in any dwelling to five in a calendar year. Five." He banged his fist on the table, rattling dishes and turning heads. "Do you know what that does to a financial prospectus based on my selling thirty-seven vacation weeks for each of the twenty-five condos in the complex?" He didn't wait for an answer. "It wipes it right out . . . wipes *me* right out. If that ordinance passes, Kincade Construction is bankrupt, and I'm left sitting on the most luxurious financial disaster in the history of this state."

Kate didn't stop to wonder why this news, which only a week ago would have pleased her no end, inspired a feeling of solicitude so strong it was hard to harness her alarmed concern into a coherent response. Questions, problems, possible solutions all assaulted her mind in a bewildering jumble.

"Can they do that? Will it really bankrupt you? What can we do?"

Matt touched her nose with his fingertip, tenderly stroking the slight indentation at the bridge. "Yes, they can. Yes, it will. And I don't know, but I love you for saying *we*."

Kate smiled back at him, all thoughts of resistance lost in her willingness of offer whatever he needed.

"Start at the beginning," she instructed, pushing her barely touched sandwich away. "What prompted Gus Rennack to introduce the ordinance in the first place?"

"Several things, actually. Supposedly to preserve the quality of life on the island, but even though the ordinance is worded in general terms, it's meant specifically to stop my project."

The years away had left Kate with large gaps in her knowledge of the island's social and political climate, but from all she'd seen and heard since she returned, the locals were surprisingly supportive of Matt's venture and looking forward to the new jobs and boost to the local economy it promised.

"Why? I mean, why now? You must have had to obtain a building permit; why didn't Rennack try to stop you then? Besides, doesn't the permit make you immune to any ordinance passed now?"

Matt only looked weary. Kate had a strong hunch that his anger and resentment had been given full rein at his lawyer's expense.

"Ordinarily, yes, but this situation isn't exactly ordinary." His lips quirked at her obvious confusion, but it was a totally humorless gesture. "I'll try to explain. The building permit doesn't specify that what I'm building is a time-sharing resort. I certainly made no secret of that fact, but the application form didn't ask about it. Maybe because the form was drawn up before the concept of time-sharing even existed—I don't know. But the permit only states that I have approval to build so many condominiums of a specified size, along with the recreational facilities . . . swimming pool, game room, et cetera. So, if this ordinance passes, my legal immunity is questionable. At the very least, it would place such a legal cloud over the project that nobody would take a chance on buying in."

"But if it was general knowledge that you planned to sell time-shares in the condos, why wasn't this effort to stop you launched back then?"

"It was, but that effort was spontaneous and easily overruled by the majority of islanders who understand the need for economic development. It wasn't as well-planned or as well-financed as this one." His half-eaten sandwich joined hers at the far side of the table. "At the root of the whole problem is a forty-six-acre nature preserve that just happens to abut my property. The Block Island Conservancy has joined forces with two other conservationist groups and convinced Rennack to plead their case."

"I get it . . . they think your development threatens the nature preserve?"

Matt nodded, his expression somewhere between disgust and disillusionment. "I spent a large part of the afternoon on a conference call with spokesmen for the Conservancy and the Audubon Society, and according to them, I'm the biggest threat to the environment since carbon dioxide was invented." His laugh was short and bitter. "How does it feel to be involved with a man who not only threatens one of the few remaining island habitats of the grasshopper sparrow but also displays utter disregard for the defenseless rockroses that grow there?"

His sadness tore at Kate's heart. She wished she could reach out and hug him, and wished that it could make things better.

"You don't strike me as a man who'd hurt a fly, never mind a rockrose or a grasshopper sparrow."

That vote of confidence earned her an honest-to-goodness smile. "That's just it . . . I'm not. I took their concerns seriously right from the start. I even altered plans and added fences and other safeguards to protect that area. But it *is* on the shoreline, so I couldn't seal it off entirely."

"You couldn't anyway. That preserve is open to the public. In fact, I remember there was a big publicity campaign at the time that land was purchased about how it was to be preserved as an area for hiking, bird-watching, photography . . . things like that." She leaned forward on her elbows, totally absorbed in her tirade. "I could see their gripe if this were a wildlife refuge, but if its purpose is to provide people with a place where they can enjoy nature unspoiled, how can they possibly object to the people who buy shares in your condos using it?"

He gave a weary shrug. "I suspect their objections are based on sheer volume. The condos will bring a couple of thousand extra people to the island yearly. I guess they feel that even if a small percentage of them turn out to be negligent or destructive, they could very quickly turn nature unspoiled into nature trampled. And the hell of it is, I sort of agree with them. I had myself convinced that the steps I took to correct the problem were sufficient, but after talking with them today . . . I'm not so sure."

He reached into his pocket for a bill and laid it on top of the check the waitress had left.

"So where's the bottom line, Matt? Are you going to fight the ordinance?"

All traces of weariness fled, and a shiver ran down Kate's spine at the ruthless look that took its place. He looked like a man who would crush a rockrose or anything else that made the mistake of getting in his way.

"I have to," he said, his voice tight and hard. "I'm too far into this to back out now."

"What are your chances of blocking it?"

"I asked my lawyer that very same question." His bitter laugh cut through the warm evening like a knife.

"And?"

"And he told me I'd rather not know."

* * *

He made an all out effort to charm and entertain her on the ferry ride home, declaring the subject of the ordinance off limits for the remainder of the night. In turn, Kate did her part to lift his spirits, and by the time his battered pickup rolled to a halt in front of the lighthouse, she was finding it hard to remember that this man, who laughingly encouraged her warbling efforts to sing on the bumpy roads coming home, and whose lightest touch had the power to transform her blood into liquid fire, was a man who had no place in her future.

He kissed her once, just inside the front door, and his hunger seemed to come straight from his soul. That morning when he'd spoken so boldly of his love for her, he had been all masculine strength. He seemed no less manly now, or any less strong, but there was an underlying need in his touch that transcended the sexual desire that sparked between them.

His fevered caresses told Kate he hungered for her in ways that would frighten her if she probed too deeply. So she didn't probe. She refused to second-guess what she felt in his arms, or question the magic that was melting the sensory input from every nerve in her body into a liquid rush with just one sweetly searching kiss. For now it was enough that they each possessed the power to satisfy the other's longings, and she willingly let Matt guide her up the stairs and out to the observation deck ringing the tower, where the amalgamation of the sea and the stars and the soft, sweet sting of desire became the beginning and end of their universe.

She woke the following morning to the feeling of something moving with whisper lightness along the shore of her breast. She let her eyes drift open to find Matt, lying on his side, entirely free of the sheet that still half covered her. His head was bent to her breast, and the morning sun glazed the rich chestnut brown of his hair with gold highlights.

"You woke me up." She smiled to let him know it wasn't a complaint and simply because she felt like smiling this morning.

At the sound of her voice he lifted his head and smiled

back at her. "Intentionally. I have a very important question to ask you."

She shivered, partly from the touch of cool morning air on skin left wet from his tongue, and partly from the warmth of the fingers playing on her thigh.

"Are you cold?" he asked.

Any chill Kate may have been feeling was incinerated in the flames that erupted inside as he rolled on top of her. "Not now." Again she was awed by the quickness and strength of her own hunger and thrilled to discover he was in the same aching state.

She felt his desire in the heated virility of his lean body, heard it ripple in his voice as he asked, "Will you kiss me good morning?"

"Is that what you woke me up to ask?"

He licked her lips, then parted them to claim a long, deep kiss before answering. "No. I woke you up to ask if you'd rather take a shower before, during, or after?"

Kate rolled her head on the pillow and arched beneath him in a seductive stretch. Eyes closed, cheeks flushed from sleep and from his titillating method of rousing her, she replied, "That's a very intriguing question. I'm going to have to give my answer a great deal of thought."

Taking advantage of her relaxed pose, Matt slid a hard, muscular thigh between hers, riding it high against the softly throbbing center of her desire. "Take your time. I'm in no hurry. And I certainly wouldn't want to influence your decision."

Kate savored the wondrous sensations kindled by the slow rocking of his thigh. Purring with contentment, she slitted one eye open in time to catch a glimpse of his good-humored expression. Then he lowered his head to her breast with an absentminded, "Let's see, where was I?" and resumed the excruciatingly pleasurable ritual of lapping and tugging she'd already learned to crave. While his hot, wandering tongue paid tribute to her softness, his hands were busy smoothing the sheet tautly over the rest of her.

Leaving her breasts glistening, he slowly kissed his way lower without removing the barrier of the cotton sheet. These were no mild pecks. He went all out, using his lips, teeth, tongue, even the soft brush of his mustache to arouse an avalanche of sensations without ever touching her bare skin.

Kate moved in delight as his tongue discovered her belly button, then gave a shuddering series of pleasure gasps as he nibbled his way down one leg and back up the other. She could feel the muscles of her stomach contract as the sheet grew damply abrasive, heightening the effect of his onslaught. The slow, sweet yearning that had been building since she opened her eyes was burgeoning now, prompting her fingers to weave themselves into the silky thickness of his hair and hold on tight.

When his roving lips reached the part of the sheet covering the softly swollen area between her thighs, her desire to play was suddenly subjugated by one much more primitive. He licked at the sheet, then nuzzled it, the feeling of his mustache excitingly tenuous as it pressed against her.

"Matt," she breathed, soft and low, drifting in a hazy realm where sensation outranked all else. "I think I have the answer to your question."

Obeying the command of her reaching hands, he slid higher, and her eyes fluttered open to stare into his. Dimly, she saw the amusement in their passion-heated depths.

"What did you decide?" he asked.

Her smile was an invitation, even though the slow rotating of his hips told her he didn't need one. "I think I'll take my shower . . . after."

"That's a real coincidence," he drawled, "because I just decided exactly the opposite."

He rolled off her and the bed so quickly, Kate had the sudden feeling she was falling and grabbed for the sheet. The next instant she was dragged to her feet and marched, sputtering every step of the way, to the bathroom.

"What do you think you're doing?" she demanded, watching him fiddle with the hot-water faucet.

"Getting ready to take a shower." He grinned over his shoulder. "With you."

"Are you deaf?" she inquired at a decibel that suggested he was. "I said I decided to take my shower after."

Apparently satisfied with the water tempterature, he climbed in and began soaping his chest in a most distracting way. "I heard you, but it suddenly occurred to me that if we waited until after, you'd be all satisfied and drowsy, and I have a busy day planned for us."

"The only thing I'm going to be busy with today is my shop . . . as soon as I take a shower—alone."

Matt let her take a whole half-step toward the door before his arm snaked out to clamp wetly about her waist and haul her into the tub.

"You're getting me all wet," she protested, loving every minute of it.

"That's the whole idea of a shower."

Kate played at struggling a minute longer. It was fun pretending to be outraged when it brought her into such provocatively slippery contact with his body.

Clamping her to his side with one arm, he aimed a generous squirt of herb-scented shampoo at the top of her head. "Wash."

She hesitated, the ultimate advantage of obeying this particular command coming to her slowly, then lifted her arms to lather up. She washed and rinsed her hair with the greatest abandon of her life. Each movement that seemed so guileless was actually carefully orchestrated to arouse. It wasn't long before Matt took the bait, and his own efforts at getting clean dwindled to a halt.

He watched, transfixed, as she meticulously soaped her small, firm breasts, the curve of her hips, then bent at the waist to tend to one long leg after the other. When she straightened and turned back to face him, Matt was eyeing the view with a smile that told her he'd changed his mind about the busy day ahead.

"You're lagging behind, Kincade," she informed him briskly. "Maybe an invigorating scrub will help."

There was no way he could miss the sparkle in her eyes as she purposefully rubbed the soap between her palms. Still, he stood there passively, smiling, inviting her to have her way with him.

She did . . . dripping glistening puffs of white foam across his shoulders and chest, then using it to paint pictures on his skin. She dabbed and feathered, her fingers wandering spontaneously in a slippery exploration of his smooth flesh and the heat and steel beneath. His chest mastered, she slid her palms lower, and behind, soaping his straight hips and the intriguing hollows where hip met thigh. By this time Matt had braced his shoulders against the tile wall, his breath coming in short pants that were the second most obvious sign of his arousal.

Kate felt her excitement feeding off his, stirring to life once more the passions he'd left unfulfilled earlier. Just as she was cursing her foolhardiness in seeking revenge with a double-edged sword, he made his move.

His hands gripped her shoulders as she bent to reach his legs. "Invigorating is not quite how I'd describe the way you're washing me."

Kate kept her head bent to hide her exultant smile at his breathless tone. "Really? How would you describe it?"

"Arousing." He was moaning now, quietly, but moaning just the same. "Exciting, stimulating...oh...you're driving me crazy."

"In that case, I think you'd better cool off."

She had one foot out of the tub and the hot-water faucet turned off before he straightened up. Hot-footing it out the door, she gleefully called back over her shoulder, "After all, we have a busy day ahead of us."

That he would exact payment for her little stunt, Kate had no doubt. But how, and how soon? She pressed her back against her bedroom door and heard the sound of the cold water being turned off, and she waited. When she finally heard his voice, just outside her door, there was an unmistakable chuckle threading through his soft threat.

"That's going to cost you, lady. How long has it been since you've ridden a bike?"

"Too long."

"Good. I'm going to be merciless. A few hours from now your backside will be as sore as if I'd given you the paddling you deserve. Dress comfortably."

The sarcastic retort froze on her lips at the sound of him vaulting up the stairs. She ought to get dressed for work, march downstairs, and tell him that that's exactly how she was going to spend the day. The logic of what she ought to do made a gloomy vestige when compared with what she wanted to do. She wanted to spend the day with Matt, wanted it with a reckless fervor she'd rather not think about.

"Let's move it, m'lady. Your two-wheeled chariot awaits."

The booming command, bellowed from the bottom of

the stairs, sent Kate scurrying for her clothes. She'd go. Just as she would relish every minute of this wonderful thing happening between them. She couldn't forget the lessons of the past—didn't want to, in fact—but she wasn't going to let them make her paranoid or rob her of this time of happiness, however brief it might turn out to be.

She would just remember to move . . . cautiously. Cautious. She liked the sound of that approach. Catching her still-damp hair into a dark gold ponytail at the back of her head, she repeated the word several more times for good measure. If the Roman candles that went off inside her whenever she saw Matt were indeed a precursor of love, then she might well be on the verge of making the biggest mistake of her life. But for a while longer at least, she wasn't going to let him in on it.

Despite the fact that she hadn't ridden a bicycle since college, Kate had little doubt she'd be able to keep up the pace Matt set. After all, how much stamina could it take to cover an island only seven miles long and three miles wide?

More than she possessed, she soon discovered.

By the time they reached Settler's Rock, on the north shore, the site they'd agreed upon for their picnic, she was more concerned with a blistered fanny than the chicken-salad sandwich Matt offered her. The patch of grass where they sat was thick and soft, yet Kate swore she could feel each knifelike blade pressing into her. After a little discreet shifting and angling, she finally achieved a modicum of comfort and nibbled halfheartedly at her sandwich.

"Not hungry?" asked Matt, unwrapping his second.

"I seem to have lost my appetite." Her voice was as stiff as the rest of her.

His grin was not without a certain amused sympathy. "Pain will do that to you."

For an instant she glared at him, ready to deny the obvious; then they both burst into laughter. He reached out and squeezed the back of her neck.

"Would you like to walk for a while? It might help loosen up your muscles."

Kate rose gingerly and pressed both hands to her aching

fanny. "Right now it feels like the only thing that will help is to have this part of my body surgically removed."

"Then you'll just have to suffer." Matt's strong hands nudged hers aside and imitated their kneading motion. "This happens to be one of my favorite parts of your body."

The massage that had started under the guise of therapy soon turned erotic.

"Relax," he directed, his voice becoming a soft croon. "I can already feel your muscles loosening up."

Kate swayed against him, completely forgetting the fact that Settler's Rock was number three on the list of ten things to see on Block Island, until a station wagon pulled up and a family, complete with four children and a dog of questionable pedigree, piled out.

"Damn," muttered Matt, reluctantly sliding his hands into a marginally more proper position. "Has tourist season started already?"

"It looks that way." It occurred to Kate to wonder how far things might have gone if they hadn't been interrupted. Never in her life had she made love outdoors—discounting last night on the balcony, which she didn't think counted as outdoors. For that matter, there'd been precious few occasions when she'd made love outside the bedroom. Acts of spontaneous passion had not been Jeff's style. Chalk up one more for Matt.

"This is Settler's Rock," announced an authoritative male voice.

Kate put a little more distance between Matt and herself and turned to see one father pointing at the stone monument nearby, one worried-looking mother, and four stepping-stone children, eyes riveted on the interlocked couple standing twenty yards away.

"What are they doing?" asked step number two.

A moment of silence, then the mother spoke up. "Tell them about the rock, Harvey."

"Right. The rock. This is where the first settlers on the island landed back in 1661."

Kate bit her lip to keep from laughing at the father's game attempt to ignore the real question, and she saw that Matt was doing the same.

"I mean them," the youngster repeated, pointing straight

at them with all the no-nonsense determination of preado-
lescence. "What are they doing?"

"Never mind," instructed his mother, throwing her husband a look that plainly said "Do something."

Matt dropped his hands to his sides, still fighting a chuckle.
"I think for old Harvey's sake we ought to push on. But
first..." He stripped off his shirt, eliciting a whole new
range of emotions from their audience.

Kate couldn't help noticing how relieved Harvey and his
wife looked when Matt did nothing more than place the
folded shirt on her bicycle seat and help her onto it. She
gave him a mental hug when he chose the shortest route
back home and for the slow, steady pace he maintained as
they passed the nature preserve that had become such a
thorn in his side. Already there were elderly couples and
families with small children strolling along the winding paths,
and Matt had to be thinking about what those narrow, moss-
bordered paths would be like a year or two from now. How
long before this small patch of timelessness, with its precious crops of rockroses and golden asters, would be rad-
ically altered or destroyed?

There seemed to be no solution, no possibility of compromise or a happy ending for everyone involved. One way
or another, somebody was going to come out of this a big
loser. For Kate, it was a shock to discover that, for all she
was idealogically aligned with the conservationists, she didn't
want that big loser to be Matt.

Through sheer willpower she managed to make it all the
way to the bluffs that bordered the lighthouse property before yelling up to Matt that she would sell her soul for one
of those lambskin seat covers she used to snicker at.

He immediately coasted to a stop, chuckling with sym-
pathy-tinged amusement. "We can stop and rest a while."

"I'm not an invalid," she snapped when he tried to help
her off the bike. Then, slanting him a sheepish look, she
admitted, "I'm close, though."

"I could ride ahead and come back with the truck for
you and the bike."

She longed to say yes and cursed the stubborn pride that
wouldn't let her. "Not on your life. Not after I made it this
far." She hitched her thumb at a giant elm they'd passed

about fifteen yards back. "My father's property starts there. That means that, technically, even if I drop dead right now, I made it home."

"It also means we won't be trespassing if we sit a while."

"*You* sit. Right now standing is an infinitely more comfortable position for me."

He took a quick step toward her, hands outstretched. "Maybe another massage would help."

Just as quickly, Kate backed away. "No thanks. With our luck, old Harvey will probably decide to show the kids the lighthouse next."

He sidled closer and tucked one finger into the unbuttoned neckline of her plaid cotton shirt. The effect of the light, tantalizing caress was instantaneous. Kate felt a tremor of nervous excitement and knew the gleaming, dark blue eyes watching her had caught it, too.

"I suppose you're right. What I feel like doing right now would probably inspire the kids to ask questions old Harvey wouldn't be able to answer."

"Don't be so sure." Her voice was strained, revealing her inner struggle to ignore the gentle thrust of his finger. "You can never tell about the quiet, studious-looking types like Harvey."

"Really? How about me? What can you tell about my type?"

The temptation of his touch was becoming unbearable. She either had to melt or put a stop to it. "That you have a one-track mind," she said, moving away.

Smiling, he fell into step beside her as she stepped over a low spot in the stone wall that rambled along the edge of the road and started walking aimlessly. The land, splendid in the vivid greens of early summer, bore fragrant testimony to her father's claim that his acreage, tucked into the southeast corner of the island, was blessed with everything nature had to offer.

Wildflowers were scattered like confetti across grassy meadows. Here and there one of the island's numerous tiny lakes—no more than natural pools, really—nestled in the shade of sturdy oaks. Beyond lay the imposing, frowning spector of Mohegan Bluffs, and then only the Atlantic, stretching all the way to Spain and forming a watery grave for the countless ships that had sunk along the rocky coastline.

"I hadn't realized how much land your folks own," Matt said. "It starts back there at the road, right?"

Kate nodded.

"And goes all the way to the coast?"

She nodded again, not quite liking the degree of interest she detected in his questions.

"How many acres do they own altogether?"

Her shrug was purposely vague. "I'm not really sure. Why?"

Watching as he traced an imaginary boundary line with his eyes, she could almost hear the wheels in his mind turning.

"Hmmm? What was that?" He didn't quite turn to face her.

"I asked why you're so interested in how much land they own."

"Because I think I just came up with the best idea I've ever had." He swung around, his grin exuberant, his eyes consuming her with a look that was both hungry and possessive. "Make that my second best idea ever."

She didn't have to ask what sort of idea it was. Though she knew it shouldn't have, it astonished her that he could be plotting another project even while his current one still hung by a slender thread on the brink of disaster.

"Well, you can forget it," she told him. "In the first place, it seems to me you've got your hands full right now, and even if you didn't, my father would never go along with whatever it is you're thinking."

A look of infuriating confidence shaped his rugged features.

"You think not?"

"I know not. He could have sold this land for house lots years ago, but he refused. If you think the Audubon Society is tough, just wait until you try selling your brilliant idea to Dad."

"How about if I told him I wanted to build something really flashy on this spot. Say, a shopping mall—two tiers, lots of high-priced shops, maybe a health spa at one end. I'll bet your father would be all for it if he thought it would make you happy enough to forget about California."

The underlying sadness in his darkening eyes made a mockery of the teasing grin. He wound one finger through a golden curl lying across her shoulder and brought it to his lips. "What would I have to build to make you that happy, Kate? What would it take to keep you here with me?"

Just you, she longed to say. Instead, remembering her vow of caution, she shrugged. "Not a shopping mall, that's for sure. Besides, what difference does it make? In a few more weeks you'll be gone anyway."

"But I'll be close by. It's a whole lot easier for me to get from East Greenwich to here than it will be to go all the way to California for my daily dose of you. But, if I have to, I'll do it. You can't run away from me, Kate."

"I'm not running, Matt. I've already told you that if things work out with the shop, I'm back to stay." Her mouth curved in a small smile. "Unless you build a shopping mall in my backyard that is. You wouldn't really do that, would you?"

The vision of how a feud between her father and Matt would rend her loyalties made Kate shudder.

With the back of two brown fingers he lightly traced the graceful line of her neck. "No, I wouldn't. As a matter of fact, Scarlett"—he switched to a lazy drawl—"I think your father will heartily approve of my plans for his land."

Despite the reminder of his unshakable business drive, Kate loved the undercurrent of excitement seeping into his eyes, the rakish tilt of his mustache as he stepped closer.

"On the other hand," he continued, "he probably won't be quite so pleased with what I have planned for his daughter."

Mr. Lonergan might not be pleased, but his daughter definitely was. She took a few steps backward, in keeping with his playful stalking, then was willingly captured between the rough trunk of an oak tree and Matt's naked chest.

He closed her eyes with his lips, then strew kisses across her forehead and temples, pausing when he reached her cheek to whisper, "I'm glad you didn't run."

"I'm too sore," she answered truthfully.

He lifted her head and looked into her eyes. His own were a glittering blue, softened by love. "I promise I'll be gentle."

He was trying to reassure her, seeking her permission, and adoration for him came to Kate in a dizzying surge. Throwing her arms around his neck, she pulled him closer. Her kiss kept him a willing prisoner for long, mutually arousing moments as her tongue sought his in an exploration that was deeper and more thorough than any that had gone before. When breath ran out for both of them, Kate was reeling with the ferocity of her desire. Leaning her head back against the tree, she gazed at him through the fringe of her lowered lashes.

"Not too gentle, I hope." She watched his smile grow bolder as he lifted her in his arms and moved a few paces to a patch of velvet grass sheltered beneath the feathery curtain of a weeping willow's low-hanging branches.

With a small sigh Kate surrendered, an eager passenger on the magic carpet of the ardent touch and heady kisses that spun them higher and higher until rapture exploded inside with all the tingling magnificence of a million Fourth of July sparklers.

Sanity returned slowly, working its way from her toes upward. She gradually became aware of Matt's hair-roughened legs entwined with hers as she lay between the heat of his body and the coolness of the earth below. Turning her head slightly, she buried her face in his thick, brown hair, inhaling its sunshine-fresh scent.

"Happy?" he asked quietly.

"Very happy."

She grinned like an idiot, thinking how insufficient a reply that really was. The feeling welling inside her surpassed happiness. It was a potent feeling, this peaceful blend of joy and satisfaction she felt lying in the arms of the man whose vibrant strength threatened to become the center of her universe.

It lingered and intoxicated, and Kate was still under its giddy spell when they stowed their bikes in the shed an hour later.

Instinctively she rubbed her bottom after climbing off— an action duly noted by Matt.

He smiled apologetically. "I suppose I'm responsible for a large part of your discomfort."

"In more ways than one," she shot back. "Under the

circumstances, I think the least you can do is carry me the rest of the way."

"With pleasure." He swung her easily into his arms and headed for the lighthouse. "Actually, I'm glad you suggested this. How many grooms get a chance to carry their brides over the threshold before the wedding?"

Kate made a show of glancing around. "Do you see a bride and groom? Where?"

"Be quiet. I'm practicing."

"Ha! Fantasizing is more like it."

"Uh-uh. But if it's my fantasies you want to discuss . . ."

"I don't! I don't! I'm sorry I even mentioned the word around someone of your flimsy moral fiber."

With Kate still snuggled against his chest, her hand firmly planted over his mouth, and both of them laughing uncontrollably, Matt opened the back door and angled his way into the kitchen.

"Oh look, Tom, it's just like that scene in *Lovefire*. The one where she sprains her ankle and the hero has to carry her back to his cabin in the woods."

"Sure, Katherine."

Kate would recognize that animated feminine voice and the indulgent male response anywhere. Trying to look as dignified as possible while sprawled in a man's arms, she turned to the man and woman sitting at the kitchen table. Smiling weakly, she ventured, "Mom, Dad . . . welcome home."

9

MATT SEEMED DISINCLINED to respond to Kate's not-so-subtle elbow in his ribs, and he continued holding her nonchalantly until her father intervened with typically dry humor.

"Son, I don't think anyone would ever accuse me of being a demanding man, but when I see my youngest daughter for the first time in almost a year, I expect a hello hug. Do you think you could unhand her long enough for that?"

A broadly grinning Matt plopped Kate unceremoniously onto her feet. "No problem, sir. We were just doing a little practicing."

Wishing her elbow were still within striking distance of his ribs, Kate ignored the surprised chuckles of her parents and gave them each a hug.

"You should have let me know you were coming home." Visions of what a more poorly timed arrival might have meant added vehemence to her words.

"Talk about the pot calling the kettle black." Her mother shook her head in a joking reproach. "If it weren't for Meg, we'd never have known you were here."

"This is exactly why I didn't tell you. I knew you'd come rushing back here the second you found out. Now I've spoiled your vacation."

"Nonsense. We've had it up to here with vacation." Her father indicated a spot about twelve inches above his head.

Her mother placed two more cups on the table and nodded in agreement. "Actually, we were calling Meg to tell her we'd decided to head home early when she let it slip that you were here."

"One of us," Tom Lonergan announced with an exaggerated nod in the direction of his slim, silver-blond wife, "was suddenly overwhelmed with inspiration in the middle of dinner one night and had to rush back home to her typewriter before it all evaporated."

Shooting the tall, still-handsome man she'd been married to for over thirty years a well-practiced look of exasperation, Katherine motioned them all to sit down. "That's not quite the whole story. I just got fed up with sharing a hotel room with a man suffering from acute baseball withdrawal."

Kate and Matt laughed as her father insisted he was not suffering from any such thing, then immediately asked Matt if he'd happened to catch the score of that afternoon's Red Sox game.

"There we were in the middle of London," her mother recounted, "the home of Big Ben, Buckingham Palace . . . and what is my dear husband looking for? A newsstand that carries *Sports Illustrated*."

The mock battle raged on, with each humorous anecdote of their trip topped by an even more outrageous one, until Kate's sides hurt from laughing. Her initial discomfort gradually gave way to a spreading feeling of contentment. More than ever the bright, airy kitchen, gilded by late afternoon sunbeams and scented with fresh-perked coffee, seemed like home. The only vaguely unsettling element in the cozy gathering was Matt's casually proprietary treatment of her— something she was sure did not escape her mother's well-trained eye for romance.

It wasn't just the way he added exactly the right amount of cream to her coffee or rested his arm along the back of her chair, with his index finger finding and grazing her shoulder no matter which way she twisted or turned. It was something much more elusive, a certain warmth in his eyes when he looked at her, the relaxed way he joined in the conversation, as if he were a member of the family.

And why not? she thought with a sudden prickle of irritation. They were certainly treating him as such. Kate's well-hidden annoyance increased with every word, as her mother regaled him with the supper menu she had planned, chiding him affectionately about the state of the refrigerator, saying it was a darn good thing she'd thought to stop at the market on the way home, or they'd all starve.

Good old Dad chimed in then, thanking Matt for some minor repairs he'd evidently taken care of with such effusive praise Kate was afraid her fingernails would puncture her palms if she had to hear him call Matt "son" just one more time. The possibility that she was actually jealous was so embarrassing that she plastered a smile on her face and forced herself to join in the conversation about how she and Matt had met before anyone noticed her sullenness.

Still, the underlying cause of her resentment niggled in the back of her mind, just as it had the day at Meg's. Matt's affection for her family, disorganized and down to earth as they were, and the wholehearted way they had taken to him in turn, undermined her own opinion of him. An opinion that, while hastily formed and based in no small part on her own past mistakes, was now all that stood between her and the irrevocable act of throwing caution to the wind.

Things only got worse when Dave, Meg, and the kids descended on the lighthouse a while later. Pots and pans rattled, dishes clattered, and corks popped in a surprisingly productive demonstration of how to turn total chaos into a dinner of spaghetti and meatballs. Through it all Matt remained impressively—or annoyingly, depending on your point of view—unflappable. He willingly lent a hand wherever one was needed, whether it was to stir the sauce or help a not-quite-toilet-trained Brian pull up his pants.

Kate was busy buttering thick slices of crusty bread when she finally got a chance for a quiet word alone with Meg.

"I see you're just as big a snitch as ever," she accused, not quite managing a look of righteous indignation.

"I did not snitch on you the time you took the dinghy out all by yourself," Meg retorted with a flush. "Besides, that was years and years ago. And I didn't snitch on you this time. It just sort of slipped out."

"Well, after it just sort of slipped out, you could have

at least warned me that they were coming."

Kate winced at the way Meg's eyebrows raised over her choice of words.

"Why on earth would you need warning?" she asked, her tone innocent, her implication crystal clear.

"It was just an expression. You still should have let me know."

"I tried. I called here and the shop a couple of times, then I guess I sort of forgot. You know, with Dave underfoot all the time now, and the kids running in and out . . ." Her expression changed from sheepish to one of sisterly nosiness. "Where *have* you been spending all your time, anyway?"

"I've been busy, running errands, checking on things . . ." Kate heard how guilty the rambling excuses sounded and shoved the tray of bread into the warm oven a little more forcefully than was necessary. "Not that it's any of your business."

Meg's smile was smug. "I guess that answers my question."

Dinner was a boisterous affair, the enthusiastic conversation overriding a rash of spilled milk and sibling squabbles. The sparkle of her mother's and Meg's eyes warned Kate that it was open season for matchmaking, and with all the subtlety of bulls in a china shop they launched an all-out sales pitch, alternating between extolling her virtues and Matt's.

Matt, predictably, reacted with pure delight, aiding and abetting to the fullest, responding to Kate's squelching looks with ones that made the air between them sizzle. Only once did Kate succumb to the childish urge to kick him under the table—when Meg mentioned what an innovative cook she was, and he laughed so hard he choked on a bite of meatball.

Even that didn't slow the action. Her mother just whacked him on the back and continued to wax philosophical about how the kind winds of fate had brought Kate and Matt together . . . just like in one of her books.

"I'm not one bit surprised, either," she informed the table at large. "I always knew it would happen this way when

Kate finally met the right man."

So much for her mother's opinion of Jeff, thought Kate.

"I only wish I could have been a fly on the wall to see the sparks flying at their first meeting."

Kate, fervently wishing she was a fly on the wall right this minute, made a game attempt to change the subject. "Dad, why don't you tell Dave and Meg about that show you and Mom saw in London?"

Before her father had a chance to swallow, his wife reclaimed center stage.

"We're embarrassing her." She smiled conspiratorially at Matt. "For all her talent and charm, she's really very modest."

To Kate, feeling the heat creeping up her neck and scorching her cheeks, the expression of thorough enjoyment curling Matt's mustache was the last straw.

"Why don't you offer to let him check my teeth while you're at it?" she demanded, tossing her fork down.

An awkward silence encompassed the gathering. Even the children fell into an unprecedented speechlessness, and Kate cursed herself for being so overly sensitive. Teasing was a way of life in the Lonergan family, and she had always been able to give as good as she got.

It was Matt who salvaged the situation. With a droll expression, he looked straight at her. "I've already checked them . . . they're perfect."

The moment passed on a wave of relieved laughter led by Kate. Mercifully, the topic of conversation shifted to other matters.

It wasn't until later, after the women volunteered to wash and dry the dishes provided the men entertained the kids, that Matt broached the subject of the impending ordinance vote.

Kate listened in amazement to her family's reaction to his plight. It ran the gamut from outrage to pledges of unqualified support, intensifying her own mixed feelings on the matter. In fact, with all of them rallying around Matt, asking questions and offering advice, she suddenly felt like the outsider. Voices raised as the discussion grew more animated, and with a sudden need to be alone, Kate slipped away unnoticed.

Only a sliver of moon and a scattering of stars illuminated the beach at the foot of the cliffs. The tide was rolling in on waves of black ink that climaxed in a foamy white spray against the rocky shore. Kate climbed down the wood frame steps to the beach and had taken only a few steps when the damp, salt-tanged air made her wish she'd brought along a sweater. She wasn't cold enough to turn back, just cold enough to wrap her arms around herself and hustle toward a cluster of boulders that promised shelter from the chill wind.

Settling her back against their smooth, damp surface, she had to laugh at the absurdity of the situation. She'd escaped from a pressure cooker into a freezer, but at least out here she didn't have to smile cheerfully while they all rallied to Matt's cause. A soft curtain of tawny hair rippled about her shoulders as she hugged her knees to her chest and wondered why their fondness for Matt rankled the way it did. She of all people should understand the lure of his charm, and, given the current status of their relationship, she probably ought to be thankful he fit into her family in a way Jeff never had. But she wasn't. It only made it that much more difficult to remember that he wouldn't fit into her future in the same easy, uncomplicated way.

Up until now, all her doubts and fears about becoming seriously involved had been single-minded, focused on the risks she would be taking. It suddenly occurred to Kate that there were risks involved for Matt as well. Maybe she wasn't addicted to a glamorous, high-priced lifestyle as he kept insisting, but was she any more right for him than he was for her? Would she be able to give him the kind of unqualified support and enthusiastic approval he would need, and deserve, in the years ahead as Kincade Construction became bigger and more successful? How could she possibly encourage him and applaud his accomplishments when, in her heart, there would always be the lingering fear that his ambition would become an obsession that would drive them apart?

"Hey, lady, you wanna get warm?"

The soft sand and rumbling tide had silenced Matt's approach, and Kate jumped a little at the deep, husky sound of his voice close to her ear. Surprise quickly gave way to gratitude when she noticed the heavy sweater he was holding out to her. She eagerly slipped her arms through the sleeves and snuggled into its bulky warmth.

"Your mother said you'd be cold." He dropped to the sand beside her. "I guess there's no time to grab a sweater when you're making a great escape."

Her chin lifted defensively. "I didn't escape."

"Ah ha, then my suspicions were correct." The familiar teasing note was in his tone, and Kate knew if it weren't so dark, she would see it reflected in his glittering blue eyes as well. "You wanted to lure me down here so we could have a few quiet moments alone."

"You've got part of it right. I did want a few quiet moments . . . alone."

She *had* wanted to be alone when she set out, but now, with him sitting so close, her senses throbbing with stomach-tightening awareness of him, she wasn't quite sure what she wanted.

"I'll be very quiet. You won't even know I'm here."

Was he kidding? "I need some time to think, Matt." She leaned away from the warm fingers that were softly touching the side of her neck, flooding her veins with smoldering warmth. "And I can't think when you're doing that."

"I'll take that as a compliment."

Kate could almost feel the power of the grin that revealed a flash of white teeth in the darkness.

With a slow fingertip, he traced the tight line of her lips. "You're worried, aren't you?"

"Yes." Such a simple answer, such a tangled situation.

"So am I, Kate. Can I talk to you about it?"

The pleading edge of his softly uttered question tugged at her heartstrings, but the last thing she wanted right now was to add a shot of sympathy to the list of things muddying the waters of her thinking.

"I think you'll be a lot better off if you talk to Dad or Dave about it. I've been living away for so long. I'm afraid any suggestions I make wouldn't be very insightful. Besides, I've already told you what I think."

"Is that your polite, circuitous way of telling me to get lost? If it is, never mind. I'll just sit here and bare my soul to this little guy." He reached out and scooped up a tiny horseshoe crab plodding its way across the sand. "Hey, fella, how would you like to hear the story of my life?"

He leaned closer to the hard, silent shell now balanced on his upraised knee. "You wouldn't like to? How about just a brief rundown of the highlights since puberty?" Again the dramatic pause. "Still not interested? Boy, I can see how you got your name. Okay, then, I'll keep it short and sweet and get right to the heart of the matter—*my* heart, to be specific."

Kate's giggle was unintentional. Immediately Matt turned to her, his expression comically stern.

"Quiet. Crabs love those corny puns. Now, where was I? Oh yes, my heart. I've lost it—to a lady who makes all the years of waiting worthwhile. And I *have* been waiting, and looking, for just the right woman for a long, long time. I always knew what she'd be like, that she'd have a sense of humor and a mind of her own. I didn't know she was going to have such nice, soft . . . Never mind, that's another story."

"You're crazy," Kate chuckled.

"You're eavesdropping," he shot back. Then, addressing the crab once more, he continued, "Anyway, now that I've found this lady, the rest of my life is suddenly coming apart at the seams . . . and I can't afford to let that happen."

Kate could feel every muscle in his body tighten. Tension invaded his light tone.

"You see, the lady in question is used to nice things . . . fancy cars, lots of pretty clothes—I'm not quite sure how to express that in crab terms—but anyway, she deserves to have all those things. I want to give her all that and more."

His short, bitter laugh came as a shock, piercing Kate's heart like shards of ice.

"Instead, just when I need to be a big success, everything I've worked so hard for is about to go down the tubes."

"You're wrong, Matt," Kate interjected. While he talked, his arm had settled around her shoulders. Now, as Kate twisted to face him, she found herself comfortably angled against his side. "Wrong about your business and even more wrong about me. Big success is what destroyed my marriage to Jeff. That kind of life is exactly what I don't want."

The strain of the past two days showed as Matt's temper exploded. "Will you please stop confusing me with your ex-husband? We're two different people, and I'm getting damn sick of doing penance for his sins. All right, he was a workaholic, and I happen to enjoy my work. That doesn't mean I would ever put it ahead of you—ahead of us—for one second."

He paused to draw a deep breath that obviously did little to cool his anger. "The man owned a string of electronics firms, for God's sake. That's very competitive, high-pressure stuff. I run one small, local construction company. Sure I dream of its growing bigger, but I'm not obsessed with it. To me, success and all the financial rewards that go along with it are only a means to an end."

He turned his head away from her, and even the powerful sounds of the sea didn't ease the agonizing silence stretching between them. Watching his hunched silhouette, Kate felt only a fierce need to banish his unhappiness, and a vague sense that she was just beginning to realize the depth of her own emotional involvement.

"We make a perfect pair, don't we?" she sighed, resting her head in the comfortable nook of his shoulder. "We each see in the other exactly what we don't want, and still we love each other."

Her first inkling that she'd uttered something earthshattering was in the sudden stiffening of Matt's entire body.

"Did you hear what you just said?" he demanded a little hoarsely.

"I—I think so, but I think . . ."

"Don't. Don't think. Not now, please. For tonight, just let me savor it. I've had enough clouds lately. I can use a little silver lining about now."

His lips danced in her hair as he hugged her even closer. "That's what I want to give you, Kate: silver linings." He stilled her half-formed protest with gentle fingers against her lips. "Not just because I think you want or need them, but because I need to give them to you."

His ragged sigh, the pensive way his chin was stroking the top of her head, told Kate he was searching for words. She waited.

"Family is very important to me, Kate, because I've

never had one." She started to sit up, but his strong arms pulled her back to the harbor of his chest. "Please, before you go conjuring up visions of drafty orphanages and bowls of porridge three times a day, let me tell you it wasn't like that. The state-run children's center was clean and warm, and the food was no better or worse than any other institution cooking. But one thing growing up in one of those places and being farmed out every Christmas and Thanksgiving did for me was forge a deep, abiding respect for families."

Kate reached up and stroked the cheek of the man, wishing she could reach back in time to comfort the little boy he'd once been.

"You know, as the years went by, and I never seemed to find someone I loved enough to marry and have a family with, I began to wonder if my notions weren't too idealistic, if somehow, unconsciously, I was afraid the real thing would never equal my dreams."

The words were spoken calmly, evenly. It was all he didn't say that lacerated Kate's soul.

"You don't know how glad I am I finally found you." Relief tingled his voice as his arms tightened around her. "I couldn't stand it if marrying me meant you had to give up the things that are important to you."

"There are no things *that* important to me, Matt." Her chuckle was laced with wry self-awareness. "I guess I can understand how you got that impression, and it did irk me when you hit the nail on the head about everything I own having a designer label." She shrugged. "I won't lie to you . . . for a while I loved all the glamour and excitement of being Jeff's wife, with a new dress for every party and a party almost every night. But I guess, like you, I was influenced by my upbringing. I wanted more out of marriage than a full social calendar. I wanted more than Jeff was able—or had time—to give."

She sought his eyes in the moonlight and held them. "No matter what else you think of me, please believe that. I'm not here on a whim, or for a little R and R. I thought long and hard before I made the move back. This is where I want to be, and if I earn enough from the shop to swing it, I'm here to stay."

"Then marry me."

It shouldn't have taken her by surprise the second time, but it did.

"I . . . you . . ." She trailed off, at a loss for words that wouldn't wound, or promise that she couldn't deliver.

"Is that a yes or a no?"

That was Matt: simple, direct. Somehow she found the strength to be likewise. "It's a no, Matt. For now, at least, it has to be a no." She drew a trembling breath, knowing even before she spoke that he would deride her for falling back on the same old reasoning. "We haven't known each other long enough to take a step like that."

"Really? It doesn't feel that way to me. Let me know how it feels to you."

The terse challenge was barely out of his mouth when he fell back on the sand, pulling Kate on top of him and holding her there with no noticeable effort. The facile display of might was intimidating, and instinctively Kate began to twist away. Her attempt was futile, easily countermanded by the firm, muscular legs that captured her flailing limbs and the strong hand that cradled her head, drawing it relentlessly closer.

All trepidation fled the instant her eyes met his. For a quivering moment they stared, absorbing each other. Even in the dim glow of the night's dainty moon she could see his expression and see that it held nothing to fear.

It was a tender assault, his invasion of her mouth. A carefully orchestrated, constantly escalating series of licks and nibbles that aroused and promised, until his tongue, warm and rough, made the possession complete. She collapsed against his tumescent body, meeting his kiss with a level of hunger only he had ever aroused, only he could ever sate.

Desire rioted within her. All else—all worry, all rational intrusions—receded as the kiss rolled on, powerful, heady. His hands stroked the length of her back, flitted provocatively over and between her thighs, then lifted to thread through the long hair that curtained their faces like moonlit silk. Kate's breath was a longing sigh when she lifted her head a scant half inch, then dipped again to kiss the hint of a smile on his lips.

"How about it, Katie? Do you always catch fire like this

for men you don't know very well?" His smile was harm-
lessly mocking. "Or are you willing to admit we're a lot
more than nodding acquaintances?"

Kate considered the question. Agreement was infinitely
dangerous, but denial was impossible. Before she was forced
to make the leap from the frying pan into the fire, Matt
shoved her off him and with one swift, rolling leap was on
his feet.

"Ouch!"

"What is it?" cried Kate, watching him thrust his hand
up under his sweater and grab his left side. What had she
read on the plane about seemingly healthy men having heart
attacks during sex?

"That damn crab, that's what."

She was laughing so hard just the act of getting to her
feet was a marvel of coordination.

"One more laugh," he warned, "and when I find him,
I'm going to drop him inside *your* sweater."

She gulped and bit the inside of her cheeks with mod-
erately successful results. "All right, I won't laugh, but I
will say that it serves you right. Poor little crab. There he
was, minding his own business, when you grab him, bore
him to death with the story of your love life, then try to
crush him. It strikes me as a simple case of self-defense."

"It does, does it? Well, it strikes me that there is a much
warmer—not to mention safer—place for us to continue
this discussion about how little we know each other." He
slipped close to kiss her lips softly. It was a lover's kiss,
thratening only its gentle familiarity. "What do you say,
Kate? My room or yours?"

"Matt, we can't," she said, thinking of her parents, thinking of how Matt always managed to steamroll over all her
objections, and half hoping he wouldn't fail her now.

"Don't be such a pessimist," he coached, settling an arm
around her shoulders and heading back toward the lighthouse. "It's late; your folks have probably succumbed to
jet lag and turned in already."

He paused just outside the back door and cupped her
chin in both palms, studying her with a searching, intent
expression. "Is that all that's bothering you, Kate? Or are
you still just as worried about us?"

She wouldn't lie. "I don't know. At this moment it feels

so right, and yet...I trusted my instincts once before and—"

"Then don't trust your instincts," he broke in, his voice firm, holding all the certainty she craved. "Trust *me*. I'm sure enough for both of us. Sure about everything. Right now I feel like I could take on the world, never mind the Audubon Society."

Kate's smile was quick and full of love, and clearly it was all the answer he needed. Pulling her near, he reached for the door. The instant it creaked open, Kate knew they weren't alone. The steady, annoying drone of a sports announcer told her that her father had found a sure cure for jet lag. She and Matt jerked apart like a couple of teenagers on their first date when the overhead light was snapped on.

"There you are, Matt," her father exclaimed. "I've been waiting for you. Come on in here and catch this instant replay."

With a helpless look back at Kate, Matt obediently followed him into the den.

Her father settled himself comfortably in his favorite chair. "Look at that." He gestured in disgust at the action on the screen. "That's his third error tonight. They should have traded the bum when they had the chance."

Smiling at the small noise Matt made—a sort of choked sound somewhere between agreement and agony—Kate accepted the inevitable. She leaned over her father's chair to kiss his cheek. "Good night, Dad."

She got a quick smile and about two seconds' worth of his attention. "Good night sweetheart. See you in the morning." Then, glancing anxiously at Matt, he said, "You're not going to turn in this early, are you?"

Kate heard the hopeful note in her father's voice, saw the tortured indecision on Matt's face, and felt a rush of love for him when she heard his answer.

"Go to bed? And miss the game of the week? Not on your life."

"All right then," said her very happy father. "Grab a chair and help yourself. We've got cheese, crackers, potato chips..."

Halfway up the stairs, Kate turned to blow Matt a kiss, smiling at the note of utter resignation in his mumbled, "Pass the popcorn, please."

10

THE SILVER BELL over the shop door tinkled merrily. Kate glanced up from the morning mail, breaking into a pleased grin as Matt strode in. Dressed in dusty work clothes, he looked adorably out of place amid the ruffled pillows and lace-trimmed quilts, and Kate thought she'd never seen a more beautiful sight. A happier one perhaps, but never more beautiful.

"Good morning."

"How could it be after such a rotten night?" His voice had a decided edge.

Kate's eyes widened innocently. "Did you have a rough night?"

"Miserable. Do you have any idea what it's like to take a cold shower at two in the morning?"

She bit her lip so she wouldn't laugh. "You didn't."

"No, I didn't," he growled. "Do you know what it's like to need a cold shower at two in the morning and not be able to take one?"

"I can't say that I do, but it seems to me you'd have had your fill of cold showers after yesterday morning."

"If I could get my fill of something else around here," he told her, stepping around the counter, his voice all honey coated, "there'd be no need for cold showers."

"Really? I never would have guessed from the way you glued yourself to the tube last night."

"I'd much rather be glued to you, and you damn well know it." He leaned to nuzzle her cheek, nibble her earlobe, then moisten the inside with the tip of his tongue. His scent was infinitely more appealing to her than the delicious fragrance from the jars of potpourri. "What do you say, Kate? Want to slip into the back room with me?"

The back room. Her drifting eyelids flew open, and she shoved him away, belatedly remembering her mother, merrily sorting stock in the back room—and probably at this very moment holding a glass to the wall.

"My mother," she gasped.

Matt angled his head to brush her stubbornly retreating cheek with his lips. "I really think it will be much more fun with just the two of us."

"Stop . . . cut it out, I mean my mother is here . . . in the back room."

He groaned. "First your father, now your mother. I haven't had this many interruptions from a girl's parents since high school." Kate didn't trust the hungry, contemplative look he was giving her one bit. "Maybe I should just sling you over my shoulder and carry you off into the sunset."

As if on cue, her mother came floating through the doorway. "That's the spirit, Matt. We need more of that kind of romantic defiance these days."

Kate rolled her eyes at Matt's gloating expression. "Please, Mom, don't encourage him. He has this problem distinguishing fantasy from reality."

"Well, someone should encourage him," retorted Mrs. Lonergan, leaving little doubt about who that negligent someone was. "After all, how often do you get an offer like that?"

"Luckily, not very often."

"See?" she rolled on, ignoring her daughter's not-so-subtle sarcasm. "You're lucky Matt is such a romantic, Kate. Precious few men are."

Matt's long arm closed around the older woman's shoulders in a quick hug. "Thanks, Mrs. Lonergan. I can see you're an excellent judge of character. No wonder your books sell so well."

They both looked so smug, beaming at Kate expectantly as if waiting for her to agree. They'd have a long wait. She propped one hand on her hip and drummed the fingers of the other on the countertop.

"Do you think you could move this little meeting of the mutual admiration society somewhere else? Some of us have work to do."

Her mother shook her head in dismay. "Imagine, Sheena Alexander's daughter, and not an ounce of romance in her soul."

"Oh, I'm sure it's there, Sheena," Matt told her, making them both chuckle with his smooth use of her pen name. "I'm just going to have to dig a little deeper. Luckily, persistence is my strong point." With amusement tugging at his lips, he gave them a broad wink and a charmingly formal farewell.

The door was almost shut when Kate remembered to get in the last word. "There's a fine line between persistence and harassment, Kincade," she shouted at his back, prompting the exaggerated kiss he blew her through the shop window.

She watched him walk away, loving that strong stride with its deceptive ambling quality that was so uniquely his. He crossed the cul-de-sac, passed the daisy-laden planter in the center, and rounded the corner before she realized she was being observed with much the same affectionate interest.

"Don't look at me that way," she warned her mother, turning to rearrange the already perfect rows of quilting thread.

"What way?" came the innocent reply.

"You know what way: as if there's something going on between Matt and me."

"Now whatever would make me think a thing like that? Just because Meg said sparks flew from the instant you laid eyes on each other? Or because the first time I saw you together you were in Matt's arms? Or because you're playing a cat and mouse game that's as old as the hills? Why on earth would I think there's something going on?"

Put that way, there didn't seem to be a heck of a lot on which Kate could base a defense. She progressed from the thread to the equally tidy display of patterns. In the quiet moments that followed she heard her mother rummaging around in the back room, fiddling with the temperamental old hotplate Kate used for heating water. When she returned with two cups of tea, she settled herself in the antique swivel rocker in the corner and picked up the conversation exactly where she'd left off.

"However, if there *were* something going on, I'd say you couldn't have made a finer choice. He's real hero material, Kate."

Kate slammed down her cup with much more passion than the harmless compliment merited. "That's just fine . . . except I don't want a hero. All I want is a plain, ordinary guy—someone like Dad or Dave."

Katherine Lonergan smiled compassionately at the wistful anguish in her daughter's voice. "Honey, where did you ever get the idea that Dave and your father are not hero material?"

"I didn't mean it that way." Kate brushed impatiently at her hair. "It's just that they're . . . well, just themselves. Ordinary." She gestured with one hand, knowing she was digging herself in deeper with each explanatory word. "I mean they're not . . ."

"They're not six feet two, with bodies perfectly proportioned to their height, smoldering blue eyes, and thick wavy hair?"

Kate smiled sheepishly at what sounded like a direct quote from the cover of one of her mother's books.

"Come on, Kate. You're too smart for that. We both know that, except in a world of pure fantasy, heroes do not always come equipped with a mass of muscles and a lopsided grin." Her expression grew playfully thoughtful, full of the sassy sense of humor that made her occasional forays into motherly advice-giving so easy to take. "Of course, the fact that Matt's musculature is strictly world class doesn't hurt any."

Kate managed to swallow the hot tea in her mouth before laughing. "I don't think mothers are supposed to make remarks like that."

"Yes, but I have a dual role, don't forget. As a professional romantic, I'm telling you Matt's body is A-1." All teasing faded from her voice. "And as your mother, I'm telling you the rest of him is even nicer."

A warm feeling of pride, strangely proprietary in nature, spread through Kate at the words of praise.

Her mother leaned back in her chair and took a sip of tea. "You're wrong if you think your father's not a hero, Kate, because he is. He's been my hero for almost forty years, since the moment we met. To me, he's sunshine when it's raining; he's strength when I'm weak. His love is the foundation that's enabled me to grow and experiment in so many crazy directions. And I hope he would say the same about me."

"But I've already made one big mistake. What if I make another one?"

"I think you're asking yourself the wrong question. So let me ask you the right one: Are you in love with Matt?"

There it was, stark, blunt, devastating. The question she had so meticulously avoided asking herself. The words had all been floating around inside her head for days, even more furiously since her slip of the tongue last night, but she'd subconsciously refused to arrange them in that special sequence that would finalize her surrender. Now her mother had gone and done it for her. She drew a deep breath, closed her eyes, then opened them to see her mother waiting with indulgent amusement.

"You don't have to tell me, Kate," she said. "But you do have to tell yourself."

"But how can I be sure?"

The softly coiffed head that had always known how to figure out the toughest math problems or exactly where to find any lost article shook back and forth slowly. "You can't. That's what makes it so much fun." Kate stared in disbelief into the laughing green eyes so like her own. "You know that fantasy world where all the heroes are brawny? Well, that's also the only place where happy endings are guaranteed. Nobody can tell you if you and Matt will have a happy ending, Kate, because that's something you have to make for yourself. All I can tell you from experience is that if you decide to accept the challenge, it makes for a wonderfully exciting, interesting life."

* * *

Kate's life suddenly exploded into the realm of exciting and interesting during the next few days. Whether or not it qualified as wonderful was definitely debatable.

Her mother thought so, along with the rest of the family. Matt walked around with a permanent ear-to-ear grin that Kate insisted violated the island's ban on neon signs. Only Kate, who suddenly wasn't able to dash into the post office or stop at the coffee shop without encountering sly, knowing smiles—not to mention questions about her nonexistent engagement from people who should know better—didn't think it was quite so wonderful.

Thanks to her mother's God-given verbosity, she and Matt had become the center of island attention during these last lazy days before the busiest season of the year began. If Matt had a self-conscious bone in his body, it didn't show. He reveled in the attention, encouraging the good-natured gossip with his open displays of affection and such an array of comical gallantries that Kate thought nothing he did would ever surprise her again.

Until Thursday morning. He burst into the shop bright and early, a gargantuan horseshoe abloom with a rainbow of carnations hanging around his neck.

Somehow she managed to swallow her surprise and the bubble of laughter that came hard on its heels. "I'm sorry, sir, but you must have made a wrong turn somewhere. The Kentucky Derby isn't run anywhere near here."

"Don't be cute. This is a traditional token of good luck." He pointed at the white satin streamer hanging around his ear, and sure enough, there in red glitter letters, was the message, *Good luck! Love, Matt.* "In honor of your opening this weekend."

"Very nice," she commented after he'd hung it smack in the front window, where it probably could be seen all the way from the ferry landing. She waited for the self-satisfied smile she knew he wouldn't be able to suppress, then wrinkled her nose and added, "Except it makes it smell like a funeral parlor in here."

Refusing to take part in a verbal skirmish, he brought her chin up to receive a kiss. His warm lips twisted across hers in that special way he had, hungry, never rushing, rocking her from head to toe. She wondered if the day would ever come when his kiss wouldn't leave her with this curling sensation in the pit of her stomach, when her heart would fail to soar at his slightest touch.

"I have to get back," he murmured, his lips still touching hers so that his mustache softly tickled with each word.

Her fingers instinctively laced at the back of his neck, binding him to her. "Mmm."

They kissed again, longer, deeper, and this time he broke away with the desperation of a man who knows his own limit. "I still have some things to take care of before the town meeting tonight, but I'll be home before five." He smiled as she stood on tiptoes to trail distracting little kisses along his jawbone. "Are you coming to the meeting with me?"

She dropped her arms and strolled over to gaze out the front window, letting him stew a bit as partial payment for the fun he'd been having at her expense all week. Outside it was another in the string of warm, clear days. Sunlight streamed through the prism hanging in the window and sent diamonds of multicolored light dancing over the bolts of bright calico. Using the tail of her shirt, she erased an invisible smudge from the glass.

"I'm not sure. I'm almost afraid you've arranged to have a brass band break into 'Here Comes the Bride' the second I walk through the door."

He snapped his fingers. "Damn. I wish I'd thought of that. Do you think it's too late to hire a brass band?" Then, grinning at her disgusted expression, he gently shook her by the shoulders. "Come on, smile. It hasn't been all that bad."

"That's easy for you to say. You haven't been on the receiving end of the balloon bouquets and the candy-grams." She looked up at him with grudging admiration. "Where did you ever dig up a heart-shaped box of chocolates in May?"

A look of supreme smugness settled over his suntanned face. "True love can work all sorts of miracles."

Laughing, she let her head collapse onto his chest. "Please, not poetry. I can't take any more."

"Poetry!" His palm slapped against his forehead. "How could I have overlooked something so obvious? How would you feel about a year's worth of calls from Dial-a-Sonnet?"

"The same way I'd feel about a terminal case of poison ivy."

"Maybe you'd prefer something a little flashier."

"Honestly, Matt, having a person of undeterminable gender, dressed as Cupid, sing me six stanzas of 'You Are My Sunshine,' while a crowd of what seemed like thousands gathered outside, was about as much flash as I can stand in one lifetime."

He planted a quick peck on the tip of her nose. "Just as long as you're happy, love."

The casual way he called her *love* caused a sweet somersault inside. She felt like smiling and asking him to say it again. Instead, she frowned up at him. "I'd be a lot happier if you'd stop wasting your money on these stunts just for the entertainment of a bunch of gossips."

Leaning back against the counter, he crossed his arms in front of him. "Why? Should I be saving my money for something special? Are you trying to tell me you have a personal interest in my financial future?"

"Not by a long shot," she retorted. Then, flipping her hair back over her shoulder, she suggested, "I guess impending bankruptcy makes a man loose with a dollar."

It was meant as a joke, but once the words were out Kate wasn't sure if Matt would take it that way or if he would think she was hitting below the belt. But the only change in his expression was a mildly interested lift of his dark eyebrows.

"Didn't I tell you? I'm not going to go bankrupt after all."

If the braided rug beneath her feet had suddenly been jerked away, Kate couldn't have registered more surprise. From the way Matt and her father had closeted themselves in the den every night this week, pouring over reams of paper, she'd assumed his predicament had gotten worse. The deepening of the lines around his eyes and the traces of worry she'd detected beneath his joking had seemed to confirm it. Now he was standing there, smiling nonchalantly at her open-mouthed surprise, telling her there was no problem after all.

"What do you mean you're not going bankrupt?"

"You don't have to sound so disappointed. When you said you prefer men without ambition, I didn't realize you also liked them stone broke."

She waved her hand impatiently. "Don't be ridiculous. It's just that I've been so worried about you all week, and now you're telling me there's nothing to worry about, and I want to know why."

He ignored the question and the slightly angry note she ended on. His eyes softened. "Were you really worried about me, Kate?"

She shrugged, trying unsuccessfully for a careless tone. "No more than I'd worry about any friend in trouble."

Blue eyes crinkling at the corners, he leaned forward and slapped her on the back. "Well, old pal, you can relax. Your father and I have come up with a strategy that's going to knock the socks off their plan to block the sale of the condominiums."

"Why is it I don't trust that gleam in your eyes?"

"You're just naturally intelligent, I guess. Do you want to hear the plan or don't you?"

"By all means."

"Okay. When you cut through all the legal mumbo jumbo and the noble rhetoric, their real objection to the condos is the fact that they're located next door to the nature preserve. So, voila: We're going to fix it so they're not next door to each other."

It was an absolutely crazy question, but since Matt and her father were the perpetrators of this great scheme, she asked it anyway. "You're going to move the condominiums?"

Matt stared at her for a second, as if playing the question over again in his mind, then shook his head pityingly. "Forget what I said about being naturally intelligent. We're going to move the nature preserve."

Kate laughed out loud. "Good luck. I think it would be easier to move the condos."

"Are you always so pessimistic, or just in matters involving me?" He helped himself to a chocolate from the box on the counter. "Stale."

"I'm not being pessimistic—just realistic," Kate told him, unable to suppress an affectionate smile as he reached for another piece of the stale candy. "You can't just up and move a nature preserve."

"Our expert from the Department of Natural Resources says we can." He held up a qualifying hand. "Let's change that . . . not move, but recreate, on the even bigger tract of land I bought from your father."

Kate's jaw dropped. "My father sold land to you?"

"If you're worrying about the property values, don't. I'm not planning on moving next door to the lighthouse." A slow smile curled his mustache. "Yet."

"He always said he'd never sell," Kate said quietly, feeling amazed and a little betrayed.

"He said he'd never sell it for house lots," corrected Matt. "And he didn't. He sold it to me with the express condition that it be maintained as a nature preserve. It really works out to our mutual advantage. I get some much needed ammunition to use at that meeting tonight, and your father gets a permanent guarantee that he'll never look out his window and see twenty-seven identical houses all in a row."

The logic of it slowly penetrated Kate's bruised consciousness. "It does sound like a perfect solution. What's going to happen to the old nature preserve?"

"If all goes as I hope, it will become the property of Kincade Construction. I'm going to propose a trade: the land I bought from your father for the land the nature preserve now sits on."

"What about the rockroses and the grasshopper sparrows?"

"As much of the natural foliage and wildlife that can be transplanted will be—and that's a considerable amount, because the climate and environmental conditions are naturally almost identical. My company will pick up the tab for all relocation costs, including whatever expert consultation and assistance is required."

"But how can they move—"

Matt's uplifted palms cut her question short. "I don't know all the details yet. Some aspects of the move are still being worked out. For instance, the birds that migrate to that spot will no doubt continue to return each season, but a group from the state university has expressed interest in studying the situation and attempting to devise a way to alter their migration pattern." He took a chest-expanding breath and gazed off into the distance with exaggerated solemnity. "Who knows? Someday it may be known in aviary circles as Kincade's Solution."

"It sounds more like Kincade's Folly to me," she retorted.

"Well, we'll just have to wait until tonight to find out, won't we?"

Deep down, Kate was relieved to hear him sounding so confident. Suddenly the town meeting she'd been dreading all week was something to look forward to, as it had been when she was a kid.

"I hope you're prepared for quite a spectacle this evening. Our town meetings are steeped in tradition. Everybody from infants to grandparents turn out, although by the time the pot-luck supper is over and a fair amount of liquid refreshments have been imbibed, not everyone makes it inside for the voting." She cocked her head and shot him a teasing look. "I wonder what effect that will have on Kincade's Solution?"

His responding smile was suspiciously weak. "Right now Kincade has bigger things to worry about."

"Such as?"

"Such as the pot-luck supper and the baked beans I volunteered you to make."

He immediately squeezed his eyes shut and hunched his shoulders as if she might hit him, which, at the moment, was a distinct possibility.

"You didn't!" she groaned, knowing even before she saw his sheepish nod that, of course, he had. "Of all the stupid . . . Baked beans, of all things. I consider a meal a raging success if I can open a can of beans without cutting my finger." She stomped across the floor, turning back to glare at him. "Whatever possessed you to volunteer me?"

"Definitely not your cooking," he said, then quickly and wisely wiped the half-formed smile off his face. "Actually I was sort of backed into it. Mrs. Abbott and some of the other ladies were in the coffee shop signing up volunteers, and they started asking me about my fiancée's cooking and—"

"I am not your fiancée!" she raged.

"Try telling them that."

"No, you try. You're the one who started this whole farce in the first place."

He glazed right over his own culpability. "Anyway, one thing led to another. You know—the typical new bride cooking jokes..." He looked at her stiffly folded arms and even stiffer face and finished in a rush, "And I ended up telling them you would be more than happy to make the baked beans."

"Well, you were right," she fairly purred. "I am more than happy. I'm furious and enraged and...I'm not going to do it." She stamped her foot, wishing his head were under it. "I can't do it."

"Of course you can." His soothing tone pumped her blood pressure up another twenty notches. As Kate watched in disbelief, he pulled out his wallet and extracted a neatly folded index card. "I have Mrs. Abbott's receipt right here. She offered it," he added quickly, seeing her eyes blaze anew.

"Good. I hope you can read better than you can hear, because the way I see it, you owe those ladies a batch of baked beans."

"Okay, if that's the way you want it." With slow, infuriating precision, he refolded the recipe card. "But I can hear their comments now: 'Boy, has she got you trained.' 'You'd better send her to cooking school before the wedding,'..."

Kate snatched the card from his hand. "That's enough. I'll do it. But you're going to help."

"With pleasure."

While she read the neatly printed recipe, he moved behind her, nuzzling the side of her neck and letting his hand trace lazy circles over the zipper of her jeans.

"Where should I start?" he whispered.

"You idiot," cried Kate, trying to twist away.

He tightened his hold, growling into her ear. "I love it when you get nasty."

"Read this." She shoved the card in front of his eyes.

"Ma Abbott's Best Home-Baked Beans," he obediently read.

"Below that," she ordered impatiently.

"Step one: Soak the beans overnight in..." His voice trailed off as the full implication of step one hit him. "You don't suppose we could just start with step two?"

If there had been an ounce of compassion in Kate at the moment, she would have returned his hopeful smile. There wasn't.

"I was afraid of that," he sighed. "I guess that means we'll have to put our alternate plan into action."

"I wasn't aware we had an alternate plan," she said tartly.

"Except where you are concerned, I always have an alternate plan." The recipe was methodically torn into shreds and allowed to flutter into the wastebasket near Kate's desk. "Good-bye Ma Abbott's Best Home-Baked Beans; hello Mrs. Pulaski's almost home-baked beans."

"Who's Mrs. Pulaski?" asked Kate, not sure she really wanted to know.

"The cook at the children's center—and the woman who's going to pull our chestnuts out of the fire."

"What are you talking—"

He shut her mouth with his, kissing her as if discovering her mouth for the first time, probing for new depths of sensation, until baked beans were far from her mind.

"I have to go," he whispered close to her lips.

"Where have I heard that before?" Her teasing had a husky, vaguely disoriented sound.

"But now I *really* have to go." He gave her one more hug, a long one that left them both hungry, then let her go with a playful slap on the bottom. "And don't worry about the beans. I have the situation well in hand."

Kate rolled her eyes. "That's what worries me."

She was still worrying that evening when they arrived at the town hall.

"I don't care what Mrs. Pulaski said; a pound of crumbled bacon and a large bottle of ketchup is not going to make fifteen cans of beans taste homemade." She slammed the truck door and reached for the beans. "We'll never get away with this."

"Spoken like a true pessimist. I'm beginning to think you may need therapy to overcome this problem."

She smiled over his shoulder at Mrs. Abbott, who was staring at them oddly from her battle station behind the buffet table.

"The only problem I have is you," she said out of the corner of her mouth, "and in a few weeks you'll be long gone."

The words, spoken without thought, hung like a thundercloud in the air between them. Kate felt a shock of pain at the realization of how short their time left together was, and she saw her pain reflected in his eyes.

Matt's hands lifted to her hair, letting it stream through his fingers like pale silk. "Don't count on it, Goldilocks."

11

ONLY THE HAZY awareness of where they were, the background buzz of children laughing and friendly chatter, kept them from completing the embrace so eloquently expressed in their longing gaze.

"Come along, you two." The cheerful voice of Mrs. Abbott pierced the moment. "Those beans are the only thing holding up the chow line."

To Kate's amazement, the improvised beans were a big hit. She gallantly referred all compliments—and requests for the recipe—to Matt, who regretfully informed them that it was a very old and very secret family recipe.

The festive supper and the first part of the meeting seemed to drag by. Kate sat restlessly, watching a speckled butterfly flutter against the window screen while the issue of whether to install guard rails along the island's main routes was debated. Despite Matt's cavalier attitude, she still wasn't convinced that his plan to relocate the preserve wasn't going to horrify the opposition forces.

Only when he left the seat beside her and strode to the speaker's podium did her sense of trepidation flee. All her senses honed on him standing there, looking taller and broader than ever. Confidence streamed through her at the mere sight of him, and when the deep, rich voice that she'd heard tease and cajole and whisper love words in her ear sounded in the crowded room, she knew without a doubt that there was no need to worry.

He held her, and the crowd, in the palm of his hand. An impression of easy self-confidence underscored his casual manner as he explained his proposal in clear, concise terms, citing facts and statistics with an authorative but never arrogant air. He spoke earnestly of what this vote meant to Kincade Construction without once seeking sympathy. He explained what he felt Seaside Arboretum could mean to the future of Block Island. And when his eyes sought Kate's over the rows of heads, and he told the spellbound crowd what the island had come to mean to him personally and professed that he would never seek financial gain from its desecration, Kate knew the irrevocable answer to the question her mother had asked.

She loved him.

Pure and simple. And risky and complicated, and the very last thing she would have chosen if choice had entered into it. Luckily or unluckily, it didn't. She sat there, watching a slow smile come to him as first one, and then many, stood to voice their support, and she knew that she loved everything about the man. She loved the way he held his head tipped to one side and crinkled his eyes when he was engrossed in listening, the way one dark eyebrow climbed to an amused peak, and especially the way he could make her whole world sparkle just by walking into the room.

How could she have been so blind to the fact that his fiery ambition was just one facet of his richly shaded personality? There was no denying he was also a caring person. Combined with all the other wonderful things she'd discovered about him—his passion, his honesty, his humor— she was suddenly overwhelmed by her love for him and the need to tell him of it.

The rest of the night seemed endless. First there was the vote—a sure thing since the moment Matt had taken the podium—then a very long, very boisterous victory celebration. By the time the last bottle of champagne had been drained and the man of the evening was permitted to say good night, Kate knew it was too late, in more ways than one, for a serious discussion about anything. At first Matt indignantly waved off her request that he hand over the keys to the truck, insisting he certainly was not "too drive to drunk." But when Kate folded her arms across her chest and planted herself between him and the driver's seat, he forked them over, muttering "Women!" in the same tone of adoring disgust she'd heard her father use a thousand times to her mother.

As it turned out, he wasn't all that drunk after all. At least he wasn't too tipsy to navigate his way across the wide bench seat and, with all the directional instinct of a homing pigeon, zero in on her breast. Kate first tried ignoring him. But even in his current clumsy state, his movements had enough residual skillfulness to send a thrill spiraling through her.

"Matt, stop it, please."

He smiled at her in the darkness, his speech slow and slightly slurred. "Why? Doesn't it feel good?"

"Too good. And I have to concentrate. I haven't driven a standard in years."

"Just relax and enjoy it. I am."

She let up on the clutch too quickly—intentionally. "Okay. It's your truck."

Amazing what tender loving concern for a ten-year-old hunk of metal and rust would do for a man's sobriety.

"Take it easy! I'll never be able to find parts for the transmission on this island." His hand found its way back to his own side as he sat up ramrod straight beside her.

Kate slanted him a bemused glance. "I thought you wanted me to relax and enjoy it?"

"For now, just drive. I'll make sure you enjoy it later."

"Promises, promises."

"Have I ever let you down before?"

"No." Hesitancy filtered through her voice. "But then, you've never drunk Block Island dry before, either."

"It only enhances my desire for you, my lovely," he drawled, leaning his head back on the seat.

It seemed it also enhanced his fatigue. By the time they reached the lighthouse, his contented snoring filled the truck.

Fortunately, the short nap and the damp night air worked wonders, and she didn't have to drag him up the front porch steps after all.

"Do you think your folks waited up?" he whispered as they reached the door.

"To greet the conquering hero?" Kate asked. "I wouldn't be surprised."

"In that case, do you think we could sit out here for a while? I'd like to talk to you about something."

"You mean a continuation of the conversation we were having in the truck before you passed out?" A trace of excitement undermined her smug expression.

"Eventually," Matt admitted. "But I want to talk first."

"That's a novel approach," she remarked dryly, letting him lead her to the wicker chairs at the darkened end of the porch.

The instant they sat down, Kate sensed his mood: a sort of nervous anticipation that mirrored her own. He reached out and took both her hands in his, and Kate smiled in the darkness at the damp feel of his palms. Then, with more fumbling moves than she'd thought him capable of, he dropped her hands and reached into his pants pocket for a small, velvet-covered box and opened it.

"Now that I'm no longer in danger of spending the next twenty years or so languishing in debtors' prison," he began in a softly hesitant tone, "will you marry me?"

The words and the sight of the simply set oval diamond glistening in the blackness had an instant chilling effect on Kate's warm glow. It had been a giant step just to admit to herself that she was in love with him. She wasn't prepared to start making promises. Desperately she searched for a way to tell Matt that without hurting him and realized there probably wasn't one.

"You make it sound as if the two things are related," she said softly, evasively. "Your financial status has nothing to do with whether or not we get married."

"Doesn't it?"

Even in the darkness she saw the hard cynicism that shaped his expression, heard it in his low, clipped tone. If Kate had sensed his nervousness a moment ago, then he was equally attuned to her resistance now. She had said no without saying it, and he had heard it loud and clear.

"No, it doesn't." She shook her head in disbelief. "How can you even suggest it?"

"It makes sense, doesn't it? At least it explains why you refuse to take our relationship seriously outside of the bedroom."

Kate crossed her arms stiffly in front of her. She could see their "discussion" disintegrating into a full-fledged, all-out scene, right here on her parent's porch. "Exactly what are you saying?"

Matt met her eyes head on and held them. "I'm saying that you've been using me—using me to spice up this little experiment in coming home again."

Yesterday, last week, maybe even this morning, she would have told him to go straight to hell, but love for him was a palpable force within her, making the hurt she saw in his eyes unbearable.

"I haven't been using you, Matt," she said softly. "I never would."

"Prove it. Marry me."

The harsh determination in his voice and eyes put her on the defensive. "You have no right—"

"I have every right," he cut in. "All the rights you gave me the first time we took each other up in my room."

"The fact that we've made love has nothing to do with any of this." She was shouting now, and her cheeks flooded with color as she remembered her parent's window just above.

His harsh laugh raked over her. "Apparently in our case, making love has nothing to do with anything, period."

She stood, salty tears trembling on the rims of her eyes. "Now you're being ridiculous. I think you're too drunk tonight to discuss this."

With agility that belied her accusation, Matt moved to block her path to the door. "I am not drunk. I may have been a short while ago, but I assure you that at the moment I am seeing things very clearly—maybe more clearly than I really want to."

The disparaging note in his voice tore at Kate's heart. "And just what do you see so clearly?"

"I see that in spite of all your belly-aching about that

empty shell of a marriage you had, it might be all you're capable of. You talk a great line about wanting more, about wanting love and commitment and family, but when the chance for it is laid at your feet, you grab any excuse you can find to toss it away."

His dark eyes held a confusing dichotomy of emotions, condemnation and pleading mingled in their unwavering depths. "You handle the physical side of things just fine, Kate. But if that's all I wanted, I could buy it anywhere, with a lot less aggravation than I've been putting up with lately."

Kate stared at him, stunned, glassy-eyed. His cruel indictment seemed to make a mockery of the love she had acknowledged with such bright promise only hours ago.

Daring to touch his arm, desperately needing that physical contact, she said, "I thought we had more than that."

"Then you thought wrong." The instant the brutal words were out, the hard look in Matt's eyes softened, making Kate wonder if the bolt of pain that ripped through her heart had shown on her face. "We have a *chance* for more. God knows I want there to be so much more, but you have to give a little. Please, Kate."

She wanted to give him everything, all she was, all she could be. She wanted to tell him about the love that had swelled her heart as she watched and listened to him tonight at the meeting. But she couldn't . . . not now in the midst of cruel words and angry accusations.

So instead she let his tensely held arm slip away from her touch. Her soft, shaky words were barely audible in the dark silence. "I'm trying, Matt. But I can't say I'll marry you. Not yet anyway."

"And what am I supposed to do while you're making up your mind?"

She knew he wouldn't permit her to duck the question. He wanted to know how he fit into her life. And except for knowing that his existence was now an integral part of her own, Kate wasn't quite sure herself.

"I guess for now we go on the way we are." Trying to escape the sight of his anguished expression, she crossed to the circle of light by the door.

"You mean we go on playing games?" he demanded,

right on her heels. "Sneaking half a night together whenever we can, with you scarcely even acknowledging our involvement by day?"

Confusion, fatigue, and pain all kept her from finding the words to tell him why she couldn't give—wasn't ready to give—all that he was asking for.

He shook his head at her silence with a short, bitter laugh that pierced all the way to her soul. "That's what I figured. Well, when you decide, let me know. It's always more fun when you know exactly what game you're playing."

Nausea gripped her as she watched him storm down the porch steps and toward the truck. The need to go after him, to tell him she was wrong, sprang from someplace deep within, and she was almost off the porch before the rational half of her brain kicked back into gear and began to give her emotions a run for their money.

She wasn't wrong. In fact, she was right. If she and Matt were to have a life together, it wasn't something she could be bullied into. And she darn well wasn't going to start off by acquiescing to his demands just to prove her love.

That decision didn't make the long sleepless night any easier. Nor did it make her any easier to live with the following day when uncertainty and lack of sleep drained all the usual pleasure out of her work, setting her even further on edge. Finally, late in the afternoon, she lost the tenuous hold on her patience and snapped at a particularly trying customer.

Meg, who was helping out during the busy afternoon hours, watched in silence as the offended woman hurled an expensive quilt down onto the counter and stomped out. Then she turned to Kate with a quelling look. "That's not exactly the way to win friends and influence people—not to mention earn a living."

Kate raked her fingers through her hair. "I know. I know." She folded the quilt and shoved it back over the wooden display bar with a rush of self-anger that only added to her tenseness. "I don't know what's the matter with me lately."

Meg's mouth quirked in disbelief. "Then you're the only one on the whole island who doesn't."

"Don't remind me," groaned Kate. "I feel like the heroine

in some stupid romantic comedy . . . except I'm the only one not laughing."

"Then maybe you should be," Meg told her flatly. "I don't blame you for being a little cautious, Kate, but there is such a thing as going overboard with it. You've got a perfectly gorgeous man who's head over heels about you and doesn't care if the whole world knows it, and instead of doing cartwheels, you nearly act as if he's got the plague. Especially this morning: You almost turned Mom's kitchen door into a revolving one trying to get out as soon Matt came down." She hoisted herself up to sit on the cutting table, obviously settling in for a siege.

"You know my motto," Kate quipped, not sure if her tartness was aimed at Meg's nagging or at herself. "When in doubt, avoid."

"So what's to doubt? Certainly not Matt's feelings."

"Ha! Right now that may be the biggest doubt of all." She flung herself into the rocker tucked in the corner and absently swiveled back and forth. "You remember how my big mouth was always getting me into trouble back in school? Well, old motor-mouth did it again."

Meg listened sympathetically to Kate's brief explanation of their heated discussion of the night before.

"Let me get this straight," she said when Kate finished. "You told Matt you didn't want to make any commitments?"

"That's right."

"And Matt agreed . . . more or less."

Kate nodded.

"And now you're upset that he seems to have accepted the conditions you insisted on?"

This time Kate's cheeks turned hot pink as she nodded. "Yes, but—"

"No, no. Don't explain," Meg cut in. "That makes perfect sense."

Kate looked at her sister in bewilderment. "It does?"

"Of course. When you're in love it makes sense to do things that make absolutely no sense at all."

"I never said I was in love," Kate snapped.

"You didn't have to. I could tell by the devil-may-care way you just threw away a four-hundred-dollar sale."

"Since when are you such an expert on love?"

"Since I read all Mom's books," Meg shot back. "So how long are you going to keep up these avoidance tactics?"

"Until I come up with a better idea."

"Maybe I should have asked how long you think Matt will put up with it."

"He doesn't have any choice," Kate retorted with the self-assurance of a woman who'd devoted a great deal of thought to the subject. "We're both busy at work all day . . ."

"That still leaves the nights."

"Not starting tonight." She reached under the counter and, with a flourish, produced a small poster announcing quilting workshops to be held evenings at Sleepy Hollow. "It works out perfectly. I tacked them all over town last week, and I've already had a few people sign up for each class." Leaning back in her chair, she propped her feet on the desk with a self-satisfied smile. "So much for my nights."

"So much for your brains," sneered Meg as the tinkling of the bell over the door drew their attention.

"Matt!" Meg hopped down from the table. "What a nice surprise. I was just leaving."

Kate lurched from the chair so quickly it went on rocking crazily without her. "You can't go now."

"I have to," Meg replied, ignoring the daggers streaming from Kate's glaring green eyes. "I . . . uh . . . promised the lady next door I'd water her tomato plants every day while she's away visiting her sister, and I'm very loyal about it."

"It's nice to know you're loyal to someone."

Meg shrugged good-naturedly at the sarcasm dripping from Kate's every word. "Yes, well, loyalty comes in many guises. Bye now."

Matt had been observing the exchange with an amused smile. Now he crossed to where Kate was standing and wrapped strong, brown arms around her. Instinctively, Kate's hands lifted to his chest, but instead of pushing at him, they clung. When he stood so close, he became her entire world. Fears and doubts paled to insignificance under the powerful magic of his touch.

With the gentlest of tugs on her hair, he tipped her face up to him. Kate was more than ready for his kiss.

"Gotcha," he whispered huskily, lowering his head by desire-heightening centimeters.

Her eyes slowly closed, top and bottom lashes meeting just as the tiny silver bell tinkled merrily once more. Kate, silently echoing Matt's soft curse, jerked free from his loosened embrace just as a tiny gray-haired lady, wearing a pillbox hat and spotless white gloves, entered the shop.

"Miss Templeton, how nice to see you," Kate greeted her former second-grade teacher warmly, smoothing her hands over her hair and tugging her shirt back into place.

Catching a glimpse of Matt's sardonic smile, she realized how guilty her behavior must look, and she confirmed the impression with a slow-spreading blush. The knowledge that her cheeks were probably as scarlet as Miss Templeton's rouged ones made her foot itch to plant itself somewhere along Matt's shinbone.

The elderly lady gave Kate a prim hug without bending her backbone so much as a quarter of an inch. She smelled of gardenia perfume, just as she had back when Kate was in grammar school.

"I intended to stop by the day of your grand opening," she said slowly, enunciating each *ed* and *ing*. "But the crowd was prohibitive, so I saved my visit for today."

"I'm so glad you did," Kate lied. "This gives us a chance to chat."

If it was possible for Miss Templeton to get any stiffer, she did, making Kate feel seven years old all over again.

"I mean talk . . . converse," she amended hastily, wishing she had the nerve to say "shoot the breeze" and really give the old bat something to raise her eyebrows over.

Miss Templeton smiled. "Your establishment is lovely, Katherine. Margaret must have been an invaluable advisor. Your sister always did have a sense of what is proper and tasteful." The logical antithesis remained unspoken.

"Meg—er—Margaret is always a big help," Kate said. *And an even bigger traitor,* she refrained from saying.

Nodding approvingly, Miss Templeton turned her sharp blue eyes to Matt. Kate felt a twinge of satisfaction to see that he, just like everyone else, straightened up and squared his shoulders under her scrutinizing gaze.

"Miss Templeton, this is Matt . . . Matthew Kincade. Matt—hew, this is Miss Templeton, my second-grade teacher." Heavens, she's got me doing it, thought Kate, hearing her obnoxiously clear speech.

"Mr. Kincade." Miss Templeton deigned to offer her gloved hand. "You must be Katherine's intended. I have heard a great deal about you, and I am happy to make your acquaintance."

With mounting alarm, Kate noted the wicked gleam in Matt's dark eyes, the dangerous twist of his mustache.

"Likewise, I'm sure, ma'am," he drawled, taking her little hand in both of his big ones. "But, I'm not exactly Katherine's intended. I'm more of her . . . shall we say, significant other, and lucky to be even that."

"Significant other?"

Through her embarrassment, it occurred to Kate that she'd never heard Miss Templeton sound quite so confused before.

"I know I've read that term somewhere," she continued thoughtfully, then broke off with eyes wide open and staring straight at Kate. "Oh dear, he doesn't mean you're . . . oh dear."

"Of course not, Miss Templeton." Over the old lady's pillbox, she shot Matt a look that promised violence at the first opportunity. "He just means we're taking time to get to know each other better before we become formally engaged, and that we're not dating any others. Insignificant others," she ad-libbed with a weak smile. "Do you see?"

Miss Templeton was a sharp old bird, and once she got over her initial fluster, Kate was afraid she'd see a great deal. Luckily, she was able to give her a ten-cent tour of the shop and send her on her way with a complimentary potholder before the schoolteacher recovered enough to question Matt any further. The gleeful look on his face told Kate that he would be only too happy to answer questions on the exact nature of their friendship.

Closing the door behind Miss Templeton with a heartfelt sigh of relief, Kate whirled to face him. "How could you say that to her?"

His shrug was infinitely casual. "How could I not? I'm tired of playing games, so I simply told her the truth."

"That wasn't the truth."

"Then what is the truth, Kate? What you told her? That we're getting to know each other better before we get engaged?"

Kate felt a flush of heat race through her as she stared

at the amused challenge in his eyes. "The truth is I haven't got time to argue with you right now. I have a beginners' quilting class starting here in twenty minutes."

"That's why I'm here," he announced, calmly watching her jaw drop.

"You can't be serious."

"About being a beginner? I'm afraid so. Although I plan on advancing rapidly." He abandoned the look of feigned innocence in favor of a taunting smile. "In fact, I plan on being adept enough by tomorrow night to sign up for the intermediate class. I can hardly wait for Thursday's advanced workshop on curved seams."

"You can't take these quilting classes," she insisted, fervently wishing the store had a trapdoor and that he was standing on it.

"Why? Just because I'm a man?" He shook his head. "Tch tch. Careful, your sexist tendencies are showing. For your information, quilting—like cooking—is not a sex-linked ability."

Kate winced at the haunting quote from her recent past.

"Besides"—his voice lowered to a conspiratorial whisper—"you can never tell about a guy who wears pink underwear."

She couldn't help smiling at that, and she tossed him the clipboard so he could add his name to the class roster. When the other registrants, all women, arrived a while later, Matt took to their fawning attention like a duck to water, making it her most interesting beginners' group ever.

She'd long ago learned that beginners are eager to start right in quilting, and she'd already prepared a small square for each of them to practice on. Matt joined in gamely, but hunched over in his chair, clutching a minuscule needle in one hand and a dainty scrap of calico in the other, he was a study in ineptness.

"Hey, teach."

Kate paused in her walk around the crowded back room to check stitches. There was only one masculine voice in the group, and only one person who'd been addressing her as "teach" for over an hour.

She swung around snapping, "Yes, stude?" without thinking.

"I think that's pronounced *stud*," he corrected to the amusement of everyone, including Kate. "And thank you very much. Now, do you think you could check my expertise in another area?"

His smile was touched with such tenderness, Kate couldn't work up even a pretense of indignation.

"Let me see it." She leaned over to examine the six stitches it had taken him forty-five minutes to execute.

"Have you considered taking up fishing as a hobby instead of this?" she asked hopefully.

"Nope. I'm really very serious about quilters." His apologetic grin was not one bit apologetic. "I mean quilting."

A collective chuckle ran through the room, confirming Kate's hunch that the motive behind Matt's fumbling participation was no big secret.

"All right," she sighed. "I'll show you . . . again."

"I was hoping you would," he murmured, leaning his head much closer than necessary to watch her fingers deftly thread the needle.

With a feeling of relief, Kate watched the minute hand of the clock inch closer to the time for class to end. When someone suggested they all stop at the tavern down the street for a glass of wine afterward, she accepted first and remembered that "all" naturally included Matt later.

Through some not-so-subtle reshuffling, he wound up in the seat next to her. At first she tried to discourage the hand that rested lightly on her leg under the table, but when he proved to be as stubborn about that as everything else, she decided to give in graciously and enjoy it. And there *was* something intrinsically enjoyable about the slightly possessive gesture, something reassuring in the intimacy of his thigh touching hers.

The small tavern was a favorite with locals and with Matt's crew, and tonight, as usual, it was filled to capacity. When a group of Matt's men standing around the bar caught sight of him at a corner table surrounded by women, they ambled over.

"Nice odds, Kincade," remarked the man Kate recognized as his foreman. "Ten women to one man. How do you rate? Or are you going to tell me this is the Monday-night sewing circle?"

A hush fell over the table at the joke that hit so close to home. Kate turned her head to look at Matt, her heart constricting at the thought of how humiliating this situation might be for him. But he was grinning, not a shred of embarrassment or tension evident on his face or in his casually sprawled body.

"Close," he drawled. "It's actually my Monday-night quilting class." A few men guffawed; a couple of others eyed Matt curiously.

One burly fellow clutching a bottle of beer shouted, "Sure Kincade, if you're taking quilting classes, then I'll dance the lead in *Swan Lake*."

The whole table of women broke into wide grins as Matt reached into his pocket and produced the sorry-looking square he'd labored on during class.

"Better dust off your tutu, Vinnie," he advised amid a tidal wave of laughter.

Kate felt a rush of admiration for Matt's strong sense of self-worth and the way he refused to waver or bend to conform to the expectations of others. The incident left her with a good feeling that made it easier when, later that night, he put a very seductive end to her new policy of avoidance.

Afterward she stared up into a pair of blue eyes as dark and gleaming as the midnight heavens visible through the skylight above. Matt lay on his side, close to her. Streamers of moonlight cascaded over him, gilding his lean, naked length and leaving half of his rugged face in deep shadows. She sighed, stretching with all the luxurious contentment she was feeling. With a reverent touch, her fingers molded to the warm, steel plane of his chest, then playfully ruffled the mat of springy hair covering it.

"I should go," she whispered without moving a muscle.

Matt took the precaution of throwing one leg over the lower half of her body. "Why?"

"My folks . . ." She let the reply trail off vaguely.

"Kate," Matt began softly. Then he paused to lift the curling tendril that lay across his pillow and bring it to his lips. "I'm sure that if your parents do discover what we're doing, they'll accept the truth; that we're old enough to make our own decisions."

"Or our own mistakes, as the case may be."

Matt immediately smiled, running his gaze over her uncovered body with enough heat to bring her from melancholy to a slow burn in less than ten seconds. "I don't know. You don't look anything at all like my idea of a mistake."

"Really?" Kate smiled back sassily and rolled to face him. "What do I look like?"

His hand reached out to stroke the curve of her hip, its roundness accentuated by her position. "You look like a living, breathing incarnation of my favorite fantasy." Warm, pleasingly rough fingertips wandered down from her hip and inward, moving with unerring precision to that part of her that yearned most for his touch.

"Would you like to know what that fantasy is?" His voice was suddenly husky.

Kate leaned into his magical caress and moaned softly. "I can hardly wait."

"Good. Because I can hardly wait, too."

His mouth claimed hers in a kiss so fierce it pushed her onto her back. He rolled with her, and Kate could feel the evidence of his impatience pressing hard and warm against her thigh.

The second time was usually slower, less urgent, but tonight, Kate realized, it would not be so. Tonight his kiss was not coaxing but conquering, and she gloried in his victory. Her mouth surrendered to his potent, rhythmic thrusts just as naturally as her relaxed legs yielded even softer secrets to his deft fingers. Her fingers streamed over his body, searching for a handhold on sanity as pleasure took her soaring higher and higher.

"You respond so eagerly, so completely," he marveled. "The perfect fantasy lover."

Kate's eyes opened wide, meeting his fully, as she strained for a moment of lucidity in this vortex of desire. "I *want* to fulfill all your fantasies, Matt. I want to be perfect for you."

Matt groaned at her breathless declaration and fell against her, laying seige to her mouth and the soft skin of her throat and shoulders. Kate recognized the barrage of kisses as branding, and she was thrilled by them. His mouth trailed lower, paying painstaking homage to her breasts. His moist lips, his teeth, and finally the wet, warm blanket of his tongue caressed their hardening centers until she was trembling with the force of the shock waves racing along her nerve endings.

"Matt, please." The words were a barely audible whimper, woven through the melody of her soft, pleasured sighs. "You're driving me crazy."

"I want to, love." Slipping lower, his kisses moistened the small swell of her belly. "I love feeling the hunger in you. You're on fire with it. I feel it burning me up, body and soul." Bracing himself up on his arms, he stared into her half-closed eyes. "Do you know what it does to me to see you like this? To hear you lose your breath at my touch? Oh, Kate, I need to know that you need me as much as I need you."

"I do, Matt. I do." Alive with the pleasure he'd given, craving the satisfaction he hadn't, her hips yearned toward him. "Maybe more."

He straightened, covering her body with his. "That's impossible. Nobody has ever needed or wanted anyone more than I want you at this moment."

With slow deliberation, he settled himself over her until his body filled hers completely. Kate closed her eyes and her mind to everything but the exquisitely slow climb to a peak of desire she'd never dreamed she could attain. Gradually the beat of their passion quickened, growing more urgent, more primeval, until fulfillment came in seemingly endless spasms of pleasure, pulsating from deep in her stomach to every cell of her being. The white-hot release was so intense it obliterated all else, save the gentle sound of Matt's voice and then his own shuddering groan.

When Matt finally moved it was only to roll to his side so they lay face to face, still entwined. As if he could never touch her enough, his fingers lightly rubbed her back.

"You see how it is with us, Kate?" he asked softly. "Do you realize how rare, how very special this is?"

She yawned against his shoulder before giving him a sleepy smile. "Special, yes . . . but definitely not rare. If anything, I'd say it was very well-done."

"Very well done," he agreed. "And very exciting . . . and very frightening."

He was watching her reaction intently, but Kate was too drowsy to bother wondering why. "Uh-uh. I wasn't frightened. Well, maybe I was a little worried at first, about my folks and all, but—"

"I don't mean frightened like that," he cut in, the impatience lacing his tone rousing Kate somewhat. "But I know it can be very frightening to want somebody, need somebody, so much that you lose control in their arms. I don't think it's ever happened to you before."

Kate drew back to her own side of the bed, suddenly getting the message that this was not just cozy pillow talk. "Maybe not..."

"I know it hasn't." His eyes refused to release hers. "You come alive in my arms, Kate. Totally, completely alive. In doing that, you abandon that ironclad control you exert over every aspect of your life. And that scares the hell out of you." He silenced her attempt to protest with a wave of his hand. "Maybe not at the moment it's happening, but afterward. I've given this a whole lot of thought, and I know I'm right. You keep telling me, and yourself, that it's my ambitious nature you're wary of, but that's just a convenient dodge. What you're really afraid of is your own loss of control, and the irrevocable fact that I hold the key to it."

It was a quiet, masculine statement of fact, and Kate didn't like having it sprung on her at such a vulnerable moment. Defensiveness shaped the host of retorts racing through her mind.

"Assuming you are right, which I seriously question, I don't see what earthly difference it makes. After all, we've already decided that whatever happens between us in bed has nothing to do with the rest of our lives." She wondered if it hurt him to hear those words half as much as it hurt her to say them.

His face remained inscrutable. "So we have. I just thought you'd like to know that in your own way you're every bit as ambitious as I am. And I think you've got some crazy notion that losing control in any way—even to your lover while he's loving you—threatens that ambition."

She clutched the sheet over her breasts. "So now I know."

"Right. And now we can go back to Lonergan's Solution."

An unsettling feeling grew inside Kate as she watched his face. "Lonergan's Solution?"

"That's what I've decided to call it. You don't want promises? We won't make promises. You don't want strings? There'll be no strings. You want things footloose and fancy free, here today, who knows about tomorrow? The quintessential summer fling with nothing but one good time after another?" His calm, unemotional tone chilled her to the bone. "Well, lady, you've got it."

12

GOOD TIMES.

Saturday morning, long, lonely days after Matt had characterized their relationship with those ambiguous words, they were still frozen into Kate's brain. Good times. Wasn't that what they wrote on phone-booth walls? For a good time call . . . She thrust the distasteful thought aside and began totaling the week's receipts for the third time.

Halfway through the first column, worry once again triumphed over responsibility, and she jabbed the paper with her pencil. The unintentional force snapped the point off and sent it flying. From across the shop her mother eyed her curiously. A moment later her cheery voice summoned Kate from the suddenly impossible task of adding double digits.

"Kate, do you think you could help this lady select fabric to make a pillow? I'll handle the register for a while."

"Of course." As she slid from the high stool, Kate smiled at the plump, middle-aged customer. "What color did you have in mind?"

"I like these." She indicated two bolts of flowered fabric. "But I can't decide which one I like better."

Kate, her back to the door, hadn't been paying attention

to the people wandering in and out. Now she jumped in surprise at the sound of a familiar gravel-edged voice close behind her.

"Take the blue," the deep, earnest voice advised the woman. "It matches your eyes."

Kate looked from the woman's suddenly flustered countenance to the smoldering look Matt was melting her with and had to choke back a chuckle.

"Do you really think it matches my eyes?" the thrilled customer was asking Matt, who nodded solemnly.

"It's exactly the same softly glowing shade." His mustache slanted above the smile Kate adored.

"Then that settles it." She turned to Kate. "I'll take enough of the blue to make a pillow." Her eyes danced to Matt. "Make that enough for two pillows."

"An excellent choice." Before Kate had time to react, Matt whisked the bolt of fabric off the table and handed it to the woman. "Mrs. Longergan over there will be more than happy to cut it for you."

"I'll be more than happy to cut it right here," Kate interrupted, taking the fabric from the woman and smiling stiffly at Matt. "I'll be with you in just a moment, sir."

Matt smiled back, apparently unconcerned by the warning glitter in her green eyes, and once more reached for the bolt of blue fabric. "I don't want you to *be* with me." His voice was pitched low. "I want you to *come* with me. Now."

The poor customer watched in confusion as they each gripped their respective ends of the bolt and held on stubbornly.

"I can't go with you now," Kate told him through clenched teeth, "or anytime soon. Saturday is my busiest day."

"Mine, too," he shot back, "but I'm still here."

"Swell." Kate jerked the fabric and gained a few inches, which Matt quickly recaptured. "But just because you decide to sashay in here after I've hardly seen you in days doesn't mean I have to drop everything and run off for more of your good times."

Dark eyebrows lowered over a mocking gaze. "So now you're anti-good times as well as anti-wealth and success."

"At the moment I'm mainly anti-arrogant, overbearing men who'll do anything to get their own way."

Impatient blue eyes locked with stormy green ones over the sea of blue-flowered cotton that neither one would surrender. As they stood, frozen, Kate was struck by the unnatural, almost breathless silence surrounding them. She glanced around to discover they had attracted quite a sizable audience for such a small shop. A hot flush of embarrassment flooded her, followed quickly by the steadily growing urge to laugh at the utter ludicrousness of their impasse. One look at Matt's twitching mustache told her he was feeling the same urge. She couldn't tell who came out with it first, but soon their rich peals of laughter were filling the room, echoed by the head-shaking, wildly applauding crowd surrounding them.

As the laughter faded and Kate still hadn't come up with a graceful way to get them out of the situation, her mother bustled over. Lifting the fabric from Matt's and Kate's suddenly eager-to-relinquish hands, she kept up a steady stream of cheerful patter as she chased them out the door.

"Now you two just run along. I'm perfectly capable of handling things here. Isn't it romantic?" Kate heard her croon to an elderly gentleman who looked as if he thought all three of them had essential components missing. "Oh, to be young and in love."

Matt's truck was parked in the narrow drive beside the shop. He slid behind the wheel and turned to her with an endearingly sheepish grin.

"I'm sorry I was arrogant and overbearing."

"I'm sorry I overreacted."

She hadn't been aware of his tension until she saw it drain from his body and relief take its place.

"God, I've missed you, Kate."

The hungry words reached out to her, and Kate hurled herself across the seat into his open arms. "I've missed you, too."

"I've been so busy getting ready for the opening tomorrow, I haven't had five minutes back to back all week."

"I understand."

"Well, I don't understand." His arms tightened around her; the kisses he strewed over her hair were tinged with desperation. "I can't stand to think about what my life will be like after tomorrow."

Kate rested her head against the rock of his chest, savoring his closeness. *Neither can I, Matt,* she longed to say. *Neither can I.* Only the painful lump of unwanted tears in her throat blocked the words.

"It doesn't have to end like this, you know," he said, the statement almost an entreaty. "With just one little word you could put both of us out of our misery."

That little word hung like a great, yawning chasm between them. Silently Kate lifted her eyes to his, watching the hopeful expectancy in them give way to an intensity of pain that tore at her heart.

"Matt, I'm sorry."

A feeling of gross ineptness swept over her as she stared at his profile, his jaw barely moving as he said, "I take it that's another no."

"I'm not saying no," she told him, gulping a deep breath at the hopeful look he turned to her with. "But I can't say yes yet, either."

His expression turned hard. "Then what are you saying, Kate? Maybe? We'll see? Dance a little faster, and I'll let you know?"

She shivered at the dark note of condemnation implicit in his taunting and summoned every ounce of her courage for what must finally be said. "I'm saying I love you."

Just saying the words out loud at last was like having a tremendous weight lifted from her soul.

Matt's quick grin of jubilation faded as he focused on her solemn expression. "At least you're admitting that much. So why won't you marry me?" His eyes burned into her.

"Because I don't take marriage lightly."

"Good. That's one more thing we have in common."

Kate wet her lips nervously, grasping for the words that could make him understand the insecurities that had been seared into her. Make him see that the problem lay with her, and she had to solve it from the inside out.

"I have to be sure this time, Matt, and that's going to take time. I know I must sound like a broken record, but we've still only known each other a few weeks."

Matt reached for her, framing her ribcage with steady hands and fixing her with a sexy look. "That's right . . . so just think how great we'll be when we've had years of practice."

"There's more to a good marriage than good sex," she snapped, shoving his hands away. "Believe me, I know."

"How could you?" he asked cynically. "You've never had a good marriage." He straightened, hunkering back against the door of the truck. "I can give you a hundred reasons why we should get married, why I *know* our marriage would be a good one. Can you give me even one good reason why we shouldn't?"

"I'll give you two. First, because I'm still not one hundred percent sure it will work, and second, because you're too damn stubborn to ease up and give me the time I need."

"I don't have the kind of time you seem to need," he countered sarcastically. "Have you forgotten my reason for being here ends tomorrow? I have jobs stacked up waiting for me. I *have* to leave, and I want you with me."

Raw anger flashed inside her. "Have you forgotten I run a business here? I have no intention of packing up and traipsing after you like some camp follower."

His look was scornfully impatient. "I wouldn't expect that, and you damn well know it."

"Do I?"

"If you don't, you should. I meant I want to know you're with me, that we belong to each other. The physical logistics can be worked out later." His voice was light and crisp, very businesslike. "I'm sure there are plenty of couples in the world who commute farther than a twelve-mile ferry ride every day."

"Oh?" The lift of her eyebrows was franky derisive. "You'd be surprised how tricky working out the physical logistics can be, Matt."

"Don't you trust me?"

"I just don't think you know what you're talking about," she said, suddenly feeling and sounding very tired. "I'm afraid that once we're married, your noble love-conquers-all speech will take a back seat to the demands of your work." The sarcastic twist she gave the last word was unintentional and unmistakable.

"Why are you so paranoid about what I do? Most women want their men to be successful, to be able to provide them with life's comforts. What the hell do you want?"

"I don't know," Kate countered furiously. "A farmer, a garbageman . . . *not* a man who wants to blaze trails, who's going to spend every waking moment plotting his next project, his next big deal."

"Are you so different?" His voice, steady, well-modulated, alarmed her more than impassioned shouting could have. "Pouring over your patterns? Planning shop layout and merchandizing strategy? I love your enthusiasm and interest in your work because it's part of what makes you you. Why can't you accept that my work is part of me?"

She lowered her eyes. "I do accept it. I just don't know if I want to live the rest of my life playing second fiddle to a pile of lumber."

He banged the steering wheel with both fists at that and sat glaring at her. "How can you even suggest that? Do you really think work is all I have in mind? Well, let me tell you, lately my mind isn't even on work when it should be. That's why I'm here now, trying to get this settled between us once and for all. This morning a snapped cable almost took a man's arm off because I was thinking about you instead of what I was doing."

Kate leaned forward, reaching out to touch his arm. "Matt, no..."

"It's all right." He pulled away from her touch impatiently. "Luckily, he was alert enough for both of us, but it scared the hell out of me. I've told you I want more in my life than just work, and I meant it. But I'm not some sixteen-year-old kid who can afford to spend months mooning over you." He met her eyes with a hard look, the look of a man who's compromised as much as he planned to. "I asked you to marry me, and I want an answer. If you insist on a long engagement... well, I won't like it, but I could take it. But I can't take any more of this... dancing on the end of all the strings you attach to your love."

The enormity of what was happening between them overwhelmed her, paralyzing her brain. Her hands reached blindly to grip his arm. She could feel the muscles in it clenched to a steely tenseness, and her words came out in a broken rush.

"I won't say yes just to pacify you, Matt. I can't... not until I'm ready. Please, can't we just take things slowly? Unmarried people can commute just as easily as marrieds, you know," she added in a feeble attempt at lightness that didn't even put a dent in his stormy expression.

He shook his head slowly, adamantly. "That's just not good enough, Kate. One way or the other, I need to know where I stand with you before I leave here tomorrow."

"And if I can't give you a definite answer by then?"

"Then I guess that's my answer."

She'd told him she needed more time; pride wouldn't let her beg him for it. But love wouldn't let her walk away without trying once more to soften his stance of marriage or nothing. "So where do we go from here?"

"I only know where I go. Right after the opening I have to leave to check out a shopping mall site in New Hampshire. After that . . ." He shrugged with a carelessness his rigid jaw said he was far from feeling. "Well, you'll be able to find me if you want me."

"I do want you, Matt." The tears clouding her vision colored her words.

Matt lifted a finger to trace the slight dent across the top of her nose. Something about the simple, lingering touch struck Kate as utterly, heartbreakingly final. "You have to want me enough to take me even though I don't come with any money-back guarantees."

Stress slammed Kate's heart against her ribs. It might as well have been an ocean separating them instead of a few inches of sunny summer day. "I really do love you, Matt."

His bitterness pierced her soul with the softness of a lightning bolt, halting midstream the trembling fingers she lifted to touch his cheek.

"Yeah, but not enough."

13

APPROPRIATELY, GRAY CLOUDS hovered over the just-waking village when Kate opened the shop early the next morning. Her twinge of concern over what rain might do to Matt's gala opening was instinctive, springing from some place deep in her heart.

Inside the shop, Saturday's hordes of browsers had left a hodgepodge of disarray, and Kate found the act of straightening and rearranging blissfully soothing. She sorted, grouped, and folded, wishing she could make her life neat and tidy again with the same easy skill. She had all the pieces—a job she loved, a man she loved and who loved her—but somehow they refused to click neatly into place. Life with Matt would be a new horizon, offering promises sweeter than anything in her past. Why couldn't she trust him—and herself—enough to reach out and grab it with both hands and a happy heart?

After months of patting herself on the back for emerging from her divorce without a trace of bitterness, the possibility that she'd also come out of it without being able to trust another man again was a shocker.

The arrival of early-bird customers, a pretty, blond woman in her forties pushing a wheelchair, provided a welcome diversion. The man sitting in the chair was also blond, tall, and muscular in a way that made his handicap seem even sadder.

"We passed by the shop yesterday afternoon," he explained, "but it was so crowded we didn't even attempt to get in . . . with the chair and all. We're glad to find you open early, before the mob descends." He tossed Kate one of the friendliest smiles she had ever seen. "You must be an early riser, too."

"Very early." Her nod had a special vehemence this morning. "Can I help you with something, or are you just looking?"

"You can probably help us with some fabric in a while," the woman replied, "but we'd like to browse a bit first."

"Take your time. I'll be around; just give a shout."

She moved to the other side of the shop and started replenishing the baskets of embroidered-satin sachets. Through the confusing swirl of her thoughts, she couldn't help smiling at the couple across the room, chatting animatedly about this quilt or that. How nice that he took such an interest in his wife's hobby, Kate thought, her smile freezing when she remembered Matt's interest had been similarly exuberant.

"We're ready whenever you have a minute."

The summons provided Kate with a lifeline from her own thoughts. She crossed to the cutting table to find bolts of fabric piled high.

"It looks like you're going to be busy," she said with a laugh, pausing with scissors in midair. "How much would you like of this yellow check?"

"None."

"Two yards."

Kate looked from one determined face to the other. "Please?"

The woman sighed in exasperation. "I say none. The green-flowered fabric on the bottom is a much better choice."

"The green is too busy to use with that brown," her husband insisted.

"Put your glasses on, Sam. The green is perfect." Then, to Kate she said, "We'll take two yards of the green."

"Of the yellow," he countered before Kate could make a move.

It was obvious the disagreement wasn't serious. In fact, the couple seemed to be thoroughly enjoying the exchange.

Kate crossed her arms in front of her. "I have a foolproof way of settling this: Who's doing the work?"

"I am."

"I am."

She eyed them both suspiciously. "Are you pulling my leg?"

"Nope." The woman laughed, slanting a meaningful look in the direction of her husband. "We *usually* work very well together."

"Except when she makes such a glaring error in judgment," Sam retorted. "Let's just buy both of them and fight it out when we get home."

"That sounds fair enough," agreed his wife. "We'll take two yards of the green *and* the yellow."

While Kate measured and snipped, Sam decided to check out the menu in the window of a new restaurant down the street. She watched from under her lashes as his wife helped him maneuver the wheelchair out to the sidewalk.

"I think it's terrific that you two share such an interest in quilting," Kate told her.

"We used to share a lot of things before Sam's accident," the woman explained without a trace of remorse. "Skiing, dancing... I guess it was just natural for us to find new things to share."

"It must be very hard for you."

The woman smiled indulgently, as if she'd heard that comment often before. "No, it's not hard. Hard was sitting in that hospital, waiting to hear if Sam was going to live or die. When the doctor told me he was going to make it, I knew nothing would ever be hard again." She stopped and chuckled. "Of course, we have more inconveniences in our lives than most folks, but I wouldn't trade it for a life without him."

Cursing the sentimental streak that always made her cry at happy endings, in movies and in real life, Kate blinked back an emotional tear. "You must be an exceptional person... to have your whole life changed that way and come out smiling."

"Honey, Sam is my whole life, or at least the most important part of it." Her voice held an unquestionable strength. "And I still manage to get in a little skiing."

She pulled a credit card from her purse to pay for the purchases Kate had wrapped while they talked. "But you know, I'd rather just sit with Sam than ski with the whole Olympic team. Funny, isn't it, how love has a way of putting things in perspective?"

Kate didn't think it was a bit funny. She thought it down-right insightful. The wisest words of wisdom she'd heard in a long, long time. After the woman left, she snuggled into the swivel rocker, propped her feet up on her desk, and tried to get a grip on the metamorphosis taking place within her.

Perspective. That was precisely the magic adhesive she needed to assemble all the bits and pieces of her future. There was a time for playing it safe and a time to go for broke, and what she and Matt had between them was so rare, so precious, it was worth taking any risk.

Like the morning sun burning through the clouds outside, her mood turned buoyant and golden. For the first time in weeks she was without doubts and fears. Arching her head against the chair's high, cushioned back, she directed a hearty gust of air at the fragile glass wind chimes above. Instantly the shop was filled with the merry sound of their movement and her heart was filled a glorious confidence that all her tomorrows would be dappled with the joy of Matt's love. Sharing a life with him suddenly seemed so easy, so inevitable.

The bell over the shop door joined the fading song of the wind chimes. She turned to see Meg stolling in and remembered that her sister had offered to help out today. The opening of the condos promised to lure unprecedented crowds to the island, and the teenage girl Kate had finally found to work part time was still learning the ropes.

"Would you like to know what they say about people who sit all by themselves and smile?" Meg asked, plunking two paper cups of coffee down on the desk.

"No, but I have a feeling you're about to tell me anyway."

"That they're either crazy or in love. So which is it?"

"Crazy or in love?" Kate mused out loud, stroking her chin in exaggerated thoughtfulness. "I think I'm a little of each. Correction, make that a lot of each."

Meg let out an exultant whoop. "Does that mean an announcement is imminent?"

"Sort of imminently delayed." Kate grinned at Meg's look of total bafflement. "I just have to announce it to Matt first."

"You mean he doesn't know?" Meg's brow furrowed. "What if he says no? Not that I think he will, but—"

"I'm not going to propose to him, you idiot," Kate interrupted. "He already did that. I just haven't told him yes yet."

"So what's stopping you? He's only ten minutes away."

"I know, but I don't want to tell him out at the site, especially today, with all those people around. I want time to explain things to him."

"What's to explain?" Meg's shrug was typically unconcerned. "You throw your arms around the guy and say 'Take me, I'm yours.'"

"It's not that simple. We've both said things . . . things that complicate the situation and need to be explained."

"I guess you know best," Meg said, but her shaking head and hesitant tone said otherwise.

With the arrival of the first ferry full of tourists, the day turned chaotic. Kate smiled and answered questions and cut fabric and rang up sales with a song in her heart that had nothing to do with her burgeoning profit margin. Wispy images danced before her eyes, smiling at her from every corner of the crowded shop. Matt, wearing only a burgundy towel and a rakish grin; Matt, all lean muscle racing beside her along the beach at dawn; Matt, at work, asleep, at play. The fleeting visions were somehow more real to her than the pandemonium all around, prompting a series of embarrassing blunders, until, after she'd shortchanged three customers in a row, Meg finally stepped in.

"Why don't you get out of here and put your body where your mind's been all morning?"

"I couldn't leave you all alone with Jenny. You need my help."

Meg's mouth twisted into a wry smile. "I hate to tell you, Kate, but as help goes, you're being a real hindrance. Consider it an act of mercy," she prodded. "Matt's probably in worse shape than you are. At least you're a happy bungler."

Put that way, Kate decided, she really didn't have much choice.

She arrived at the site in a mood of giddy anticipation, hardly recognizing it from the last time she'd been there. Where there had been piles of loam and hulking machinery, now there was rolling green lawn and shrubbery that bore the mark of professional landscapers. The atmosphere was festive, combining all the best elements of a carnival and a down-home family picnic.

Clowns in full regalia cavorted amid long tables laden with food. Kids of all shapes and sizes frolicked on the plush carpet of grass and stood with watermelon juice trickling down their chins as they munched and waited their turn on one of the frisky ponies high-stepping around an improvised corral.

Like a Geiger counter tuned to detect one thing only, Kate searched for Matt and found him standing off to one side with a small group of men. Taking a deep breath through lips that had been chewed raw in the last few days, she started toward him, noticing as she drew closer that her brother-in-law, Dave, was also among the group.

That was as much as she did notice. Her eyes drank in the sight of Matt as if he were cool, clear water in the midst of desert heat. He looked magnificent, arms folded across his broad chest, one hip leaning slightly in a deceptively casual stance that she knew belied a will of sheer iron. How many of his business associates, Kate wondered, had been fooled by that laid-back demeanor into thinking Matt Kincade was easy game? His khaki slacks and dark blue open-necked shirt fit him to tailored perfection, though she was certain they had come right off the rack or, even more likely, been ordered from the battered sporting-goods catalogue kicking around in his truck.

"Aunt Kate!" a tiny voice called out in excitement. "Look, Daddy, Aunt Kate is here."

Daddy wasn't the only one who looked. Matt turned to face her as well, and suddenly his stance didn't seem all that casual. Kate could swear he had caught his breath, just as she had, the instant their eyes met. Time and her wobbly legs seemed to move in slow motion as she trekked the final few steps to his side. In those elongated seconds she studied every detail of his face with protective attentiveness.

The lines at the corners of his eyes were deeper this morning, and she detected a tired droop of his mouth, despite the tentative half smile that formed and faded only to form again. His perusal of her was no less thorough. Every nerve in her body felt touched by him. There, in the middle of clowns and ponies and heaven knew what else, she felt suddenly dizzy at the force of her need for him—emotionally, physically, in ways she'd never dreamed she could need someone.

And he was so close. Only a few steps and a few words away. The words had been planned and rehearsed, honed to perfection on the slow drive out here. Now she stopped in front of him and, smiling nervously, said simply, "Hi."

"Hi." He tilted his head to one side, and his eyes narrowed quizically. "What brings you way out here?"

Kate's pulse quickened. Please let that be hope she saw so carefully shrouded in his eyes. "I think you have something that belongs to me."

It wasn't quite the eloquent speech she'd planned, but at least it grabbed his attention. As the others turned politely away, the familiar traces of amusement filtered into his dark blue eyes. "Really?" he drawled. "What's that?"

My heart, my future, all right there in the palm of your hand. Out loud, very properly, she said, "A box. About this size." Her hands marked off small, square dimensions that made his eyes sparkle and an honest-to-goodness smile curve the mustachioed mouth she loved. For a minute Kate thought he was going to grab her right then and there, but he just shrugged nonchalantly.

"Oh that. I left it back at the lighthouse." Then, his smile taking on a hint of challenge, he said, "How would you like to take a little ride to get it?"

A ride—precious moments alone with him away from all this delightful madness. "I'd like that."

He reached for her hand, and at the same instant Kate felt someone tug on the leg of her slacks.

"Aunt Kate, Aunt Kate," the persistent little voice floated up to her. "Guess where Uncle Matt's going to take us."

She smiled down at Kathleen's eager little face. "Where

is he going to take you, honey?"

"For a balloon ride. Right, Uncle Matt?"

"That's right, Kathleen," Matt assured her, looping an arm around Kate's waist. "Right after I take your Aunt Kate."

With unmasked skepticism, Kate eyed the red and white striped hot-air balloon moored nearby. "Matt, is that thing really safe?"

"You're about to find out firsthand."

To the delighted hoots of all in the vicinity, he lifted her in his arms and hoisted her into the cushioned basket. It was too deep to vault back out, or she would have.

"What do you think you're doing?" she demanded, her voice rising on a note of panic.

"You said you wanted to go for a ride." He fiddled with the collection of gadgets and levers above their heads.

"I meant a *ride*—on wheels, not in a floating bread basket."

"Shhh. I have to concentrate. I've never soloed before."

She gripped the coiled-rope handles, her eyes wide with alarm. "You mean you're driving this thing?"

"The wind drives it. I'll just sort of control our altitude."

The words were followed by a slight, very disconcerting hissing sound from the balloon above. A couple of young men wearing "Balloonists Do It Airborne" T-shirts quickly untied the ropes from the stakes, and they were off. It was an eerie sensation, watching the ground fall away beneath them in absolute silence.

"Wasn't that takeoff smooth?" Matt asked proudly.

Kate had to admit it was, but the mention of takeoff brought to mind that old axiom: What goes up must come down.

"How do we get this thing to land?" She tried to sound interested, not panicked.

"By letting the air out."

Kate shut her eyes against the terrifying picture that presented and kept them shut while the balloon drifted slowly higher.

"Isn't that view something?" he asked in a marveling tone.

"Breathtaking," Kate replied.

"Kate." His hands on her shoulders were as gentle as his voice. "Open your eyes."

"I can't. I'm afraid I'll get sick."

He chuckled. "Anyone who can eat chili dogs on a rocking ferry isn't going to get sick in a balloon on an almost windless day," he said in pointed reference to her choice for lunch on their trip to the mainland.

She opened her eyes obediently and peered over the side, at first cautiously, then with mounting wonder. The island was a variegated patch of green standing out dramatically against a crystal blue sea. As Kate got caught up in the magic of the ride, her apprehension ebbed. The air was clear and warm, with only the slightest breeze ruffling the gleaming waves of Matt's hair. Watching him throw himself into the ride with a boyish enthusiasm that was every bit as much a part of him as the hard-nosed business sense that drove Kincade Construction, Kate felt a rush of desire.

"Matt," she said, moving to stand behind him, her hands sliding sensuously around his waist. "Do you suppose those T-shirts are right?"

"What T-shirts?" he asked distractedly.

"The ones that say balloonists do it in the air."

Laughing, he twisted around to stare into her dancing eyes. "I'd sure love to find out, but not in the three minutes we have left before landing."

"Only three minutes?" She rubbed her cheek against his back, wishing the magical ride would go on forever.

He nodded. "Thereabouts. I think we're as close as we're going to get to where I want to go."

"Where's that?"

"Right about there."

He pointed over the side of the gradually descending basket to a spot Kate recognized as part of the land parcel her father had sold to Matt. The landing was accomplished with the same gracefulness as the takeoff. When the deflated balloon was secured, Matt lifted Kate from the basket. Still holding her in his arms, he started walking toward a slightly wooded area on the far side of the clearing.

Kate pressed her cheek against his chest, loving the warmth of him, the safe, steady sound of his heartbeat.

"I didn't know you liked hot-air ballooning," she remarked, playfully twirling a tuft of bronze hair at the open neck of his shirt. "Tell me some of the other things you like."

"No way." He bent his head to nuzzle the neck she arched for his pleasure. "I'd much rather have you fumble around and discover them for yourself."

Kate closed her eyes to the faint smile on his lips. Why had she thought long, belabored explanations would be necessary between her and Matt? She had come, and he had welcomed her. It was that simple, would always be that simple for them. They passed through the shady grove of trees, a world of soft shadows and cool air scented with evergreens. Somewhere out of sight, tiny forest creatures rustled the low-growing bushes; in the branches above, birds spoke, their voices clear and sweet.

On the other side of the grove sunlight greeted them once more. Matt walked on, carrying her effortlessly past dogwood trees in full pink and white splendor and clusters of blueberry bushes, their fruit still hard and green. When he finally put her down it was in the middle of a patch of sweet-smelling clover, high on a cliff overlooking the spot where the Block Island Sound flowed into the Atlantic Ocean.

"I wonder why on earth you wanted to come way out here," she said, slanting him a knowing look.

His lips dropped to hers in a quick, hard kiss. "Not for the reason you're thinking . . . at least, not just yet, anyway. You're really going to marry me?"

"Well, I was hoping to get a closer look at the ring before—" Her heart melted at the appeal in his eyes. "Of course I'm going to marry you. Do you think I would have climbed into that wicker contraption with you if I wasn't planning on for better or worse?"

"You didn't exactly climb in," he reminded her, laughing when she stuck her tongue out in retaliation. "Do that again."

Kate shook her head at the provocative challenge. "No way. Not until I find out why we had to land on this exact spot if not so you can further compromise my virtue."

"I'll get around to your virtue," he promised. "First, how would you like to live on this exact spot?"

"In the middle of the nature preserve? How romantic— just you and me and the squirrels and countless bird watchers."

"Stop," Matt ordered, amusement edging his voice. "Before you put your foot any farther into your mouth, you might be interested in knowing that the nature preserve ends on the other side of that grove of trees. The acre or so of land you're standing on is mine . . . soon to be ours."

"You really mean it?" Kate hurled herself into his arms. "Oh, Matt." A sudden thought pierced her joy. "What about your work?"

"What about it?"

Kate recognized the desire-husked tone of his voice and the lazy look in the eyes lingering on her mouth. "How will you be able to manage if you're living over here?" Without giving him time to answer, she shook her head firmly. "No, Matt, it's not fair. I love you even more for suggesting we live here. I know you're doing it for me, but I can't let you. I couldn't be happy living here, knowing the burden it would put on you, thinking of you shivering all by yourself on the ferry every day all winter long—"

"Whoa, slow down." A smile teased the corners of his eyes. "We haven't even dug the foundation yet, and you've already got me suffering from pneumonia. Actually your speech leaves me feeling a little unworthy. You see, I'm not exactly noble enough to suggest we live here on the island. What I have in mind is a kind of compromise."

"I live here, and you live on the mainland," she quipped. "How innovative."

"*That* is absolutely out of the question," he warned, trying hard to look ferocious. "I won't be a stickler about 'love, honor, and obey,' but I definitely want to include the part about 'whither thou goest, so goest I' in our marriage vows."

Kate smiled at him sweetly. "I hate to tell you this, Matt, but I think that quote is from a greeting card, not the marriage ceremony."

He shrugged. "You're the one who wants to be innovative." As Kate watched, a look of worry shadowed his eyes that had been laughing a moment ago. "Would you consider living here half the time and in my house in East Greenwich the other half?"

The idea suited Kate perfectly, spendidly, beyond mere words. "I'd love it!" she exploded, and then the world was spinning around her as Matt lifted her off her feet in a wild, swinging hug. "I love you," she told him when her feet touched ground again. "And I'm going to love your house in East Greenwich. Of course it might need, shall we say, a woman's touch. You know, new drapes, carpets..."

Matt was wincing painfully. "Do you think we could go slowly with all that? This deal with the nature preserve qualifies as an unforseen expense—a big one—and it's put a temporary dent in the financial holdings of Kincade Construction... not to mention Kincade personally."

Kate looped her arms around his neck and pressed closely against him. "Lucky for Kincade I'm not the kind of woman who needs expensive clothes and cars to make her happy."

It pleased her that he had the decency to look admonished. "It *will* make my immediate future that much easier."

She lifted herself into his kiss eagerly. His lips moved on hers slowly, tenderly, breaking away only to whisper words of love in her ear.

"Would you like to see our island house now?" A tempting invitation drifted across his features.

"By all means." Kate put her hand in his and followed until he came to an abrupt halt about thirty paces away.

"This will be the front porch," he announced grandly. "I know it's not stylish, but I want one anyway... with a swing." He tugged her along with him through a maze of imaginary rooms: living room, dining room, his office, ending with the kitchen. Letting go of her hand, he marked off the invisible walls with his feet. "I'll plan for lots of windows, so that while you're cooking you'll be able to look out and see any of our kids who might happen to be playing in the backyard."

"I don't cook, remember?"

Nothing, it seemed, could dim his thousand-watt mood. "Okay, you can look out the windows while I cook." He walked back to her and rested his arms lightly on her shoulders, his look a heartmelting blend of love and concern. "Are you really sure now, Kate? No matter what I said yesterday, I don't want you to come to me with doubts."

She loved him even more for that ultimate sign of his flexibility, and her eyes told him more than words ever could. "I have no doubts about our love for each other."

"And all the rest?" he persisted.

Slanting him a smile that promised much, she said, "The rest will just add spice to our lives."

She felt his breath come warm and fast as she tiptoed a step closer and began to sway back and forth against him. "I do have a question though. Does this place have a bedroom?"

"Mmm-hmm." He lifted her and lowered her gently to the cushion of fresh-scented grass. "And we just happen to be standing in it."

Eyes dazed with love and mounting passion, Kate smiled up at him. "How clever of you to put the bedroom in the kitchen."

"That's the best part of being married to a contractor."

She felt the warm mist of his whisper against the upper swell of her breasts as the neckline of her top was inched lower.

"Wrong, Matt." Her voice was husky with laughter and more. "That's not *quite* the best part of being married to a contractor."

And pulling him down beside her, she showed him what was.

WONDERFUL ROMANCE NEWS!

Do you know about the exciting SECOND CHANCE AT LOVE/TO HAVE AND TO HOLD newsletter? Are you on our *free* mailing list? If reading all about your favorite authors, getting sneak previews of their latest releases, and being filled in on all the latest happenings and events in the romance world sounds good to you, then you'll love our SECOND CHANCE AT LOVE and TO HAVE AND TO HOLD Romance News.

If you'd like to be added to our mailing list, just fill out the coupon below and send it in…and we'll send you your *free* newsletter every three months — hot off the press.

☐ *Yes, I would like to receive your free SECOND CHANCE AT LOVE/TO HAVE AND TO HOLD newsletter.*

Name _____

Address _____

City _____ **State/Zip** _____

Please return this coupon to:

Berkley Publishing
200 Madison Avenue, New York, New York 10016
Att: Irene Majuk

HERE'S WHAT READERS
ARE SAYING ABOUT

Second Chance at Love.

"I think your books are great. I love to read them, as does my family."
— *P. C., Milford, MA**

"Your books are some of the best romances I've read."
— *M. B., Zeeland, MI**

"SECOND CHANCE AT LOVE is my favorite line of romance novels."
— *L. B., Springfield, VA**

"I think SECOND CHANCE AT LOVE books are terrific. I married my 'Second Chance' over 15 years ago. I truly believe love is lovelier the second time around!"
— *P. P., Houston, TX**

"I enjoy your books tremendously."
— *I. S., Bayonne, NJ**

"I love your books and read them all the time. Keep them coming—they're just great."
— *G. L., Brookfield, CT**

"SECOND CHANCE AT LOVE books are definitely the best!"
— *D. P., Wabash, IN**

*Name and address available upon request

Second Chance at Love®

All of the above titles are $1.95

Prices may be slightly higher in Canada.
